*f*OUR IN THE *a*FTERNOON

Ann Marie Bertola, Michelle Reiff,
Anne- Marie Dardis, Caroline Wilders,
Magdalena Fainé, Mariana Ibáñez,
Margaret Mullan

Consecrated Women in the Regnum Christi Movement

Published in the United States of America by
Circle Press Hamden, CT

/spirituality/,/women's role/./women's issues/,/decision making/,/
Catholic Church/,/vocational discernment/,/biography/

All quotations from the Bible are taken from the Ignatius Holy
Bible (Revised Standard Version: Catholic Edition), published by
Ignatius Press, San Francisco

Printed in the United States of America
Second Impression 2004

ISBN: 0-9743661-0-2

$\mathcal{W}$e dedicate this book
to all those who helped us with
their prayer, example and support
as we discovered and accepted our call
to consecrate our lives totally to Christ
in the Regnum Christi Movement.

*C*ontents

*f*OREWORD

Fr. Anthony Bannon, LC

*I*f you start with the theory and limit yourself to it you are apt to spend much time trying to plumb the mystery and nature of the vocation - unsuccessfully.

Like all stories of love, the vocation cannot be grasped by the mind only. Since it is a matter of love, our connection with it, what gives our true understanding, is our heart. Or perhaps we should speak of intuition rather than something as plodding as understanding. Intuition, with its sudden spark of light, sudden unexpected vistas and simple, satisfying clarity is much more like the Author of the vocation, God himself, the God of surprises, than the drudgery of statistics, hypotheses and confirmations on which we place so much stock today.

Looking at examples, the phenomenology of vocation, if you will, sparks these necessary intuitions. And for those who are searching for their own way in life, such intuitions can be determining in finding it, although further reflection will have to develop and deepen the first "eureka!"

The stories in this book allow us to pierce the experiences of the women who speak, and discover in them the essentials of the vocation. The seeking heart, the patient Shepherd who knows and calls each sheep by name, the creating and creative God who made us for himself and comes out to meet us in such varied ways, the timid, searching, resisting, weak human heart yet capable of being so generous and total in its self-giving once it discovers the touch of love, the absolute conviction based on faith, nourished in prayer and the Sacraments, the desire to serve.

Read on. Let these women introduce you to the world of God's extraordinary action in the ordinary things of life. Let their experience speak to your heart so that you may discover his workings in your own life and encourage others to do the same. And may their generosity spark something similar in your soul also.

Fr. Anthony Bannon, LC.

Fr Anthony Bannon, LC

*I*NTRODUCTION

*J*ohn leaned back in his chair. He was tired. His eyes and hands ached after a whole day hunched over the desk writing.

That would have to do for today.

If he could, he'd continue tomorrow. He rolled up the scroll and wiped his stylus.

"I'm not as young as I used to be," he said to himself. His old age was daily more obvious, not only to him, but also to the whole community of Christians at Ephesus. Miriam, a poor but good woman, had taken to cooking his meals. Cephas, her son, had taken to accompanying him wherever he needed to go. They insisted on doing it, although John tried to discourage them. And John was grateful.

He pushed open the door and eased himself onto the doorstep. The sunset was more than worth the poor area where he lived: it blazed over the sky, its glory heralding the first notes of chill in the evening. Winter was slowly creeping its way into Ephesus. The sun slid further and further down the mountainside, until all was blanketed in a deep purple, broken only by the stars above and the lamplight from houses.

Thoughts - prayers filled his mind. No number of years could ever erase the memories. They were as vivid in his mind as hot coals, and he tended them as carefully. He must write. He knew he must write. God asked it of him, as did the Christians. Nonetheless, how could he describe in words what Jesus was like to those who had never known him, seen him, heard him preach? All those years he had spent with Christ as a young man — walking from town to town, sleeping in open fields, talking into the late hours of the night — he never thought he'd have to tell anyone about them. Him? John? The youngest fisherman of the Sea of Tiberias, and the youngest disciple in that band that had followed Jesus? The goodness, the bravery, the uprightness, the gentleness, the wit which made up Jesus' personality all seemed nearly impossible to convey in their fullness.

"God is love."
That was the only accurate and complete description that came to John's mind.

It was late and the chill had settled into the hills, but John would stay a while more before turning in. The lights below dimmed as those in the heavens shone the brighter.
"God, you are love for me; you have always been love for me, since the beginning."

Since the beginning... It was that first moment John was thinking about now. It was that first moment he had been writing about before he came outside.

He remembered Andrew, his friend, and James his brother; they had long since gone to rest with God. It was with Andrew that he had met the Christ for the first time, that day they were with John the Baptist at the river. "Behold the Lamb of God," John had said, as a man passed by. The Lamb of God? The Promised One of Israel? They had both looked at each other, and without really knowing why, rose up and began to follow the figure to whom the Baptist pointed.

The elderly John chuckled. Oh, and he and Andrew had tried to be discreet as they argued in whispers about who would speak first to him. Yet if he didn't ask quickly, the Christ would be lost in the crowd. John broke stride with Andrew and walked swiftly to catch up to Jesus, trying to think of something to say. It was the Lamb himself who turned around and addressed his young pursuer:

"What do you seek?"

The eyes that met John's carried the universe, the voice echoed experience and wisdom, and the question caught John completely off guard. Fumbling for an answer, he replied not fully aware of the words that came out:

"Sir - where do you live?"

John felt like striking himself on the forehead. 'Idiot!' he'd scolded himself. 'What kind of a stupid question is that?" He was about to open his mouth again, when he saw the face of the Christ. Jesus smiled at John and then at Andrew, now beside him. He smiled at them both, and the smile was love.

"Come and see."

They followed him. They spent the whole day with him; they spent their whole lives with him; they would spend eternity with him.

It was late. The old man grasped the door post to pull himself up. Come morning he would regret having stayed out for so long in the night air. Inside, dinner awaited him on the table. Miriam had come in and left it without him noticing. It would wait for tomorrow. The letters? They would wait for tomorrow as well. But one thing couldn't be left for tomorrow.

He walked over to his desk and pulled out his scroll. There was a detail missing. Some would think it insignificant, but to him it had value beyond compare. Holding the paper up to the oil lamp's fine flame, he found the place he was looking for. John uncapped the inkwell, took up the stylus in his stiff hands and added this brief note to his text:

… they came and saw where he was staying;
 and they stayed with him that day;
it was about four in the afternoon.
(John 1:35-40)

*W*ELL *W*ORTH *W*AITING *f*OR

Ann Marie Bertola

"*M*om, you're never going to believe this!"
I stormed into the kitchen fuming. I'd had it. This was the last straw. I could handle criticisms and smart jokes about Catholics from another seventeen-year-old, but from one of my own teachers right in front of the whole class—never! "You're never going to believe what Mr. Ross said in sociology class today. He said Catholics really believe that the Eucharist is Christ's body."

Startled, and not sure whether to take her enraged teenager seriously, my mother answered slowly:
"Ann Marie, honey, we really do believe that."

I was totally staggered. My Jewish sociology teacher knew more about Catholicism than I did.

*S*UNDAYS AT THE *B*ERTOLA'S

"Ann Marie! Todd! We're late!"
I looked across the room I shared with my older brother. We were seven and eight years old at the time. He was sitting on the floor, shirtless and shoeless, running his Hot Wheels across the carpet. I wasn't in much better shape. Reluctantly I hopped off the top

bunk and landed with a thud.

"We can't keep God waiting!" Mom called down the hall-way.

I pulled on my socks and began rummaging through our common closet for a matching pair of sneakers.

"Come on, Todd," I said in what I knew would be un-heeded motivation as I tossed a pair his way. "Mom said." Todd defiantly threw one of the racecars under the bed, picked up the shoes and began to dress. The weather outside was beautiful, as it usually was in Santa Catalina, the L.A. suburb where we lived. It would have been a great day to ride bikes or go to the playground. Going to Mass was not the way Todd and I would have chosen to spend our Sunday mornings.

Nonetheless, we were all baptized, made our First Holy Communion and squirmed in Mass every Sunday. This was my experience and interest in religion up to my sophomore year of high school.

*f*AILED *a*TTEMPTS TO *C*ONVERT A *C*ATHOLIC

My high school had the reputation for being the most ethnically diverse high school in Los Angeles County. Our unify-ing creed was tolerance and respect. No one culture or way of life was better than another; all religions and beliefs had some aspect of truth—this was the basic philosophy the school promoted and the students stuck to.

So, I was Catholic. And my friends, for the most part,

were Protestant. So what? All religions were basically the same, right? We all worshipped the same God, didn't we?

All of a sudden, in tenth grade, it did make a difference. My friends, who up to that point had been as religiously sedentary as I, started to commit themselves more to their faith. Jesus Christ, and the churches they belonged to, began to take on a big role in their lives.

Zealous to make a "true Christian" out of a poor, unfortunate Catholic like me, my friends gave me sermons encouraging me to "really accept Jesus." Catholics, they told me, aren't true Christians. We aren't really saved. We are all headed for eternal condemnation. I was horrified—not because I was hell-bound, but because I couldn't believe my friends would dare break the decree of tolerance. Didn't they know that was the biggest 'don't' in the book? Since when had I ever criticized their religion?

Nonetheless, I swallowed a lot of their anti-Catholic arguments. I still remember a conversation I had with my best friend, a non-denominational Protestant, during our lunch break one day at school. As we carried our trays to the outdoor tables, she said:
"We had the most awesome service last Sunday, Ann Marie."
"Oh, really," I replied, looking around to find the rest of our friends. "What did you do?"
"It was on the beach," she said. "The coolest part was that we had orange juice and doughnuts for communion."
Scandalized, I set my tray down on the table and looked at her in puzzlement.

"You did what? Can you really do that?"
Not surprised by my 'ignorance', she said authoritatively:
"It's not what it is that's important, Ann Marie, it's what you put into it."
It sounded logical.
'Hmm, well, that makes sense,' I thought to myself.

Some of the other kids I associated with, however, weren't so friendly or diplomatic; in fact they were hostile and insulting about my faith. Even though I had very little doctrinal knowledge, their remarks infuriated me. They might be right, they might be wrong, but who did they think they were to make fun of my religion to my face?

One particular episode vividly stays in my mind. Driving home one night with my friends, we passed by a Catholic church. On the lawn, white light illumined a crucifix. It was absolutely beautiful.
"These dumb Catholics," snorted the driver. "They keep Christ on a cross. Don't they know he's risen?"

I felt my jaw clamp shut. My face began to burn. But I had nothing to answer him with.

The turning point came during my junior year. It was during Lent, on a Friday. Amanda, a friend, had invited me over to her house for a Mexican dinner her mom was making. I graciously declined with the excuse that it was Lent and I couldn't eat meat. The truth of the matter was that I didn't want to go at all. Her parents were fallen away Catholics, now Evangelicals, who always gave me a hard time about the faith when I was at their house.

"Don't worry," she told me, "my mom can make you something different."

It seemed rude to turn her down, so I ended up going. Things started getting uncomfortable the minute I sat down to eat my vegetarian nachos. Out on the back deck, Amanda's parents fired off anti-Catholic accusations at me. What was I supposed to do? Apostatize? Tell them to get off my case? Burst into tears?

I glued my eyes to the plate, and as soon as it was polite enough for me to leave, I thanked Amanda for inviting me and headed for the door. I didn't bother to tell her parents good-bye. Let them think I was a rude little Catholic girl – it would just confirm their prejudices.

As I drove out of the sub-division, I shook myself over and over. Why had I even gone? Who did those people think they were? Why did I not say anything? But what could I have said? I could still feel Mr. Luna's glare and hear the scornful tone in his voice. Catholics, he was convinced, worshipped Mary.

"What could be farther away from the truth than that, Ann Marie?" Beside him, Mrs. Luna nodded her head in agreement. "Is there any place in the Bible where Jesus tells us to worship anyone but him? If you Catholics can find one, then let me and all the other Christians of the world know because we'd be really interested. I'd hate to think that we misunderstood him when he said 'you shall have no God besides me.' But it seems pretty clear to me, Ann Marie. I don't know why the Catholic Church doesn't think so. "

Red light.

Were these people serious? I thought to myself. Catholics worshipping Mary? Since when? I had been a Catholic for sixteen years and I didn't once remember having participated in a Mary-worship ceremony. If such ceremonies existed, then they certainly weren't advertised in the parish bulletin or announced after Mass.

Green light.

I eased out into the intersection, waiting for a chance to turn left.

"Jesus," I prayed. "What are you trying to tell me? If the Catholic faith is right, then show me, because I don't know how much more of this I can take. "

By the time I had pulled into my driveway, I was decided. I would resolve this issue. I was going to study Catholicism, to learn everything I could about it and find out if it was true or not.

THE STORY OF FATIMA

Reading was one of my least favorite activities. I did it only when absolutely necessary. However, a few days after the Mexican dinner episode, I went to the local Catholic bookstore to stock up on reading material. Not having any real idea of what I wanted, I made my selection based on thickness and cover design, paid the cashier and walked home.

Every night after I'd done my homework, I'd lie on my bed and read. I was interested, very interested, but while these books provided some understanding, they still weren't the power punch I was looking for. The miracle I sought turned up in the place I least expected: the garage.

Saturday afternoon I did what I always did — chores. This particular afternoon I was cleaning out the garage. All sweaty and grimy, I sorted through the boxes of camping gear and old dishes. As I shoved aside a pile of newspapers with my foot, a little blue book caught my eye. I wiped my forehead on my sleeve and picked it up. On the cover was a drawing of Our Lady. She was standing on a cloud. Three children knelt down before her, rosaries in hand. 'The Story of Fatima', read the cover. I sat down on the pile of newpapers and started to read. Then, the miracle happened. I didn't have a vision or an ecstasy, but I actually began to enjoy what I read, an experience which up to then was completely foreign to me. The little, illustrated pages flowed like water through my fingers. I read it from cover to cover, then went back and read it again. Something about it all — Our Lady, the innocent children — made it like a homecoming. This was the religion I wanted, one of love and gentleness, not the rigid fire and brimstone, saved, unsaved, maybe saved God presented in the Protestant fellow-ships.

I carried the book up to my room and set it on the dresser. I had the certainty of a prayer being answered. Maybe I didn't know everything yet, but I knew that what that book told me was true. Mary really did come down to earth, and she only appeared to Catholics. There was a proud satisfaction I relished in that thought.

Take that, Mr. Luna.

From then on I started to treasure all things Catholic — Mass, the rosary, statues, Catholic churches, votive candles. I prayed the rosary daily, and went to Mass as often as I could convince my parents to lend me the car. Anything new I learned fascinated me.

God Plants the first Seeds of My Vocation

It amazes me to think that all of this happened during my sophomore year. Between September and May I had undergone a complete spiritual reconstruction. Now that the iron was hot, God decided to strike, and it was at Mass one Sunday that he laid the first blow.

"Good morning everyone. I'm Sister Angela Donovan, the Vocational Director."

What? A nun? A real one? Expecting the typical "after Mass announcements," I was taken aback as I listened to this fifty-something woman tell the congregation about her experience as a missionary in Africa, about the decline in vocations, about the money needed to support retired priests and religious. I hung on her every word.

My knowledge of religious life came from what I had read in the lives of the saints. I envisioned the consecrated life as a life of absolute holiness and perfection, reserved for an elite few. I never considered the possibility for myself because I knew I wasn't worthy; I wasn't special enough. But could I be a nun? From what Sr. Angela said it seemed like the Church was sending out an "All Points Bulletin" practically begging for vocations.

'The Church needs vocations,' I thought. 'Of course I'll give my life for her.' I had fallen so much in love with what it meant to be Catholic and I had seen how the Church was suffering. I was willing to do anything to help.

"I'm going downtown on Thursday. There's going to be a display or a conference or something about being a nun and I want to check it out."

My friend's eyes opened wide. She looked at me, stupefied, then turned her eyes back to the road.

"Well," she said disdainfully, "if that's what makes you happy."

Surprised by her reaction, I concluded it was best to keep my mouth shut and keep the whole thing a secret.

Yet the Vocations Day left me with more questions than answers. I passed by the booths belonging to different religious orders, told the nuns that I was interested in knowing more and left my data with them. I got the impression, though, that no one I spoke with knew how to direct me. I didn't leave with anything solid and no one ever got back to me. After that, the idea of having a calling to consecrated life filed itself away under 'possibilities'. I knew only that I wanted to give my life for the Church. Somehow.

_M_AJOR _a_DVANCEMENTS

That was how I found myself studying theology.

"What on earth are you going to do with a theology degree?" was a question I often met up with among family and friends. Um. I had no idea. But I'd tucked away some advice a priest had given me: "Whatever you major in, make sure it's something you like, because you'll be spending your life in it …" The only thing I wanted to dedicate my life to was the Church. How? I was still waiting to find out. God hadn't stuck a road sign on my path that said: Ann Marie, this direction. I didn't even see his track marks. I was following his lead blindly, not realizing he already had a plan that, little by little, he was revealing.

Everything else was working out. I'd found a Catholic college that was close to home. I'd met Matt, a real Catholic guy, who I started dating. It was all fitting in. Maybe.

God had other plans. The summer before I was going to enter university I went to a Catholic Charismatic conference in Los Angeles. My mom had met the Charismatic Movement some years prior and it had brought both her and my father closer to the Church. I wandered through the rows of displays and bookstands. 'Franciscan University of Steubenville.' Nope, I wasn't interested and I wasn't in the mood for a sales pitch. I wandered by, pretending not to notice the stand or the young man behind it. But when I had made it to the end of the aisle and turned back, he was staring straight at me. I was foolish enough to make eye contact.

'Great,' I thought, 'Now I have to talk to him.' I tried to

be polite as I listened to Jeff tell me about how great the student body was, the amazing faculty, how the Blessed Sacrament was reserved in seven different locations on campus. I was impressed but didn't let it show. I had other plans.

"That's nice, but I'm already planning to study theology at another Catholic university. Thanks, though."

Later on that night I received a phone call.

"Hi, Ann Marie, you probably don't remember me and it probably seems surprising that I'm calling you, but I have to tell you something." It was a nun I had met at one of the stands at the conference. "Jeff, from Steubenville, told me that you're planning to study theology at ————. Maybe it's none of my business, but I feel it's my duty to tell you that over half the theology majors from that university end up becoming Protestants."

Her words were like a punch in the stomach. I was stunned. I loved my faith too much to risk losing it or getting a cut-price version of it. But now what was I supposed to do? My thoughts went back to Jeff and everything he had told me about Franciscan University …

*D*ISCERNING — THE *P*LOT *T*HICKENS

Anything that could have been a problem — money, friends, family — ended up in my favor, and I arrived at the university nervous and excited. College life at Steubenville far surpassed my highest expectations. It was everything I could have ever wanted. I was so used to fighting for my faith; now, immersed in all things Catholic, my faith flourished. And I began to reconsider the item I'd filed under possibilities: my vocation. Many students were discerning a vocation and the university even offered discernment activities: talks, retreats, and so on. I went to almost everything.

I wanted a vocation, but I came to the conclusion that I must not have one. From what I'd heard, God was the one to give a vocation, the person called "saw it," or "felt it," or "knew it" and responded. I didn't see, feel or know anything, least of all, what a vocation was even supposed to look or feel like. And even if I ever were called, how was I supposed to know if it was real or just my imagination? For as much time as I dedicated to discerning, I could never get any fireworks to go off, any bang or boom that left me with the certainty beyond doubt of 'Ann Marie, this is the God-given sign. You have a vocation'.

Still Waiting for a Sign

"Lord," I pleaded as I knelt alone in the chapel, "why aren't you calling me? I want a vocation so badly."

It was early evening in the Bronx. Through the open windows in the chapel I could hear kids shouting to each other in the streets as the bass of a booming car stereo resonated off in the distance. Every so often on school breaks, my girlfriends and I would go to visit different religious orders. This particular weekend we had gone to visit the Sisters of Life in New York. Looking back, I can't believe we actually did this, but at the time it seemed so normal. The sisters were friendly, holy, and very hospitable, but the "click," "sparks," or "sign" I had so much hoped to feel was nowhere to be found. I was heartbroken.

"God, if the Church is suffering for lack of vocations and I'm here offering myself, why won't you take me?"

That Sunday night, I concluded God simply hadn't given me a vocation to consecrated life. I knew I didn't deserve one anyway, but it was still hard to swallow.

All right. I would get married — but not before I had spent some time as a missionary. With this idea in mind I went to a job fair during my last semester at college. I was hoping to find a good way to put my soon to be theology degree to good use for the Church. Among the many groups present at the job fair was the Regnum Christi Movement. One of my closest friends was a Regnum Christi member, so I decided to check out their stand. The woman representing the Movement was like none I had seen before. She was consecrated; she was friendly; she was obviously very in love with Christ and the Church. As she told me about Youth for the Third Millennium, a Regnum Christi apostolate, I burned with enthusiasm. YTM organized Catholic door-to-door missions, something I had wanted to put together for years. When I was living in L.A., at least every other week a Mormon or a Jehovah's Witness would come knocking at our door.

"When are Catholics ever going to do something like this?" I would ask myself. YTM missions were what I had been looking for and I couldn't wait to get involved.

The consecrated woman invited me to go to a Holy Week retreat in Rhode Island to begin planning and learn more about the Regnum Christi Movement. Speaking about it with my roommate later I told her:

"I'm not too sure if I want to go. After all, it's my last Easter here at Steubenville, I don't even know these people all that well, and, besides, I have absolutely no money."

Her advice was profoundly simple:

"Ann Marie, as long as God keeps opening doors in that direction, take it as a sign that he wants you to go through them."

God couldn't have opened the doors any wider. A group of girls from the university were going, so I wouldn't be there among strangers and a van from Michigan was going to pick us up on the way to Rhode Island — that solved the money problem.

As soon as I walked in the front door, surrounded by the flurry of welcome and a pile of suitcases, I felt right at home. Everything about the place: the people, the atmosphere, the chapel, the talks ... they all seemed to fit. But I told myself:

'Don't get your hopes up, Ann Marie. You know you don't have a vocation.'

But when I learned about the coworker program, a chance to give a year or two of full-time service to the Church through the Regnum Christi Movement, I knew that that was the missionary work I was looking for. I would be back in the summer to start.

AM I MISTAKEN, OR WAS THAT A CALL?

May came and my YTM friends and I were in the final stages of planning our first mission. The Saturday before the big day we had a retreat for all the missionaries. The priest, Fr. Anthony Bannon, LC, based his meditations on the Gospel of John, chapter one, the call of the first apostles.

As I sat listening to the meditation he gave, I heard Christ's invitation to the apostles in my own heart:
"Come and see."
"Lord, what are you getting at?" I asked, "I thought it was already decided."
Then, during Mass, the Gospel reading was taken also from John, chapter fifteen.
"I am the vine, you are the branches… as the Father has loved me, so I have loved you… remain in my love."

Was this an invitation?

I saw something that I'd never seen before. Christ was offering me a choice — married life or a life consecrated totally to him.
"Both are good, Ann Marie," I felt him say, "and you can choose whichever one you like, but I want you to know that what I'm offering to you in consecrated life is something I don't offer to everyone."

I had once heard someone say:
"The moment God asks something of you is the same moment he gives you the grace to do what he's asking." I saw the sign, I saw him asking – and I embraced it.

"I'm going to the candidacy," I told the consecrated after the retreat. I had expected her to jump up and down and get excited. Instead she told me:

"All right, Ann Marie, let's take things as they come. Just be open to God's will."

"I'm going to the candidacy," I told my parents. I wasn't sure how they would react. It would surprise them, I thought.

"Oh yes, Ann Marie, we were expecting something like this."

Expecting it? How? Asking them to borrow the car to go downtown for the Vocations Day five years before was the first and last time I had ever mentioned the word "vocation" in their presence.

Learning to Walk in faith

"Defensive" is the adjective that described me during the first week of candidacy. Nobody was going to force anything on me. This vocation was between God and I, and no third party would get in the way.

I opened up as I discovered that every element of the candidacy was geared towards finding God's will. But why, after seven whole days did I still not see clearly if God really wanted me?

"I've never asked you for a sign before, Christ."

I walked down the long driveway leading up to the formation center. I had gone outside to pray my rosary because the landscape was so beautiful — wildflowers, trees, the Atlantic Ocean visible in the distance, but I began to think of my family, my life, my friends. Why was I here and they weren't? Why had God preserved me? Why had he given me so much? Why did it seem that I was special to him?

I needed to know. I couldn't be kept in suspense any longer. The struggle had to end; I wanted to see plainly what God wanted for my life.

"I've never asked you for a sign before, Christ, but if you want me to be consecrated, turn my rosary to gold."

It had happened to other people, people I knew. If it would just happen to me ….

"Just make my rosary turn to gold, that's the only sign I'll ever ask for."

"Ann Marie," I heard Jesus' voice in my soul. "I could make your rosary turn into a bird if I wanted to, but what more signs do you need that I haven't already given you?"

Was he serious?

"Wait a minute, Jesus. You really mean this? This is for real?"

Yes.

This was for real. This was more real than any sign.

"I think God is calling me," I told my spiritual guide. "But how can I be 100% sure?" Her answer took me for a loop.

"You're never going to be 100% sure. God never gives 100% certainties."

"What do you mean?" I asked.

"Think about it, Ann Marie. If you knew for sure beyond a shadow of a doubt that God wanted you consecrated, what would you do?"

"Get consecrated, of course."

"Right, but you'd do it because you knew that you had to, that there wasn't a choice. God's will would be so clear that to go against it would be blatantly wrong." I looked at her, puzzled, so she continued: "In other words, you'd feel obliged, not free. Freedom is a condition for love. God wants us to choose him because we love him, freely, not because we think we've got no other choice. That's why he always leaves a little space of uncertainty, so we can fill in that gap with love."

"Oh," I said. I nodded. I understood.

"Make a leap of faith. You choose him, and once you've done that, you'll see how he confirms that decision."

The five weeks of candidacy that followed were like summer camp to me. I was in heaven and happier than I had ever been in my entire life. September 1st, the day of my consecration, couldn't come soon enough.

But the weeks leading up to that day weren't all smiles and sunshine. I had told Christ yes and wasn't about to turn back, but leaving behind my life, my family, and my own expectations became a painful reality I would have to learn to accept.

"Can I really do this?" I asked myself. "How can I hurt the people I love so much? My mom's done so much for me all my life and this will be so hard for her."

When I flew back to L.A. to say goodbye to my family, I still had a six hundred-dollar debt from college. How could I pay it? I was a week away from making a promise of poverty. I had never asked my parents for a substantial amount of money before and they had never given me money that I hadn't earned doing extra chores around the house.

"Don't worry, Ann Marie," they reassured me. "We'll take care of it." I was grateful, but I still felt bad about it — it wasn't like they had that kind of money just lying around. Still, what else could I do?

Later on that evening I went to visit my old parish priest. He had known me since I was a child and was elated about my decision.

"Come with me; I have something for you" he said, leading me to his office. "We have a parish fund for vocations and you've finally given us a chance to use it. Take this." He handed me a check for five hundred dollars.

"Father, I can't accept this," I protested in disbelief.

"You can and you will," he answered firmly and smiled.

I also went to visit my grandma before heading back to Rhode Island. As I kissed her goodbye she stuffed some money into my hand like she had done on other occasions. I wasn't about to look at it with her standing right there, but when I got in the car, I discovered I was holding a one hundred dollar bill. Six hundred dollars, just what I needed.

THE POT OF GOLD

"I promise to live in poverty, chastity, and obedience."

At last. At last. On September 1, 1996, after so many years of interior unrest, as I pronounced my promises of consecration, peace filled my soul. My heart heard with a certain, yet unexplainable security:

"This is what God wants, Ann Marie. This is his will,"
My eyes remained fixed on the small crucifix I held in my hand.
"I'm consecrated," I thought. "I am totally yours."

⥽

God's path is easy to trace in hindsight, and he makes it
easy to follow in the present if we look at life with faith. He has
his plan, his ways, his will for bringing us to find him. Regardless
of the path he plotted out for me, and the circumstances he per-
mitted me to go through, today, having discovered my vocation,
the only thing I can say to him is thank you, and the only thing I
can do for him is promise to live every moment corresponding to
the unmerited love he has shown me.

*M*OTHERS *K*NOW *B*EST

Michelle Reiff

I was just coming in the door after finishing my three to eleven shift at the hospital when the phone rang. It was my dad, which was very unusual. He usually let Mom call, and besides, it was 12:00 midnight.

"Michelle, Mom's in the hospital."

"What happened? What's wrong?"

"I'm at the hospital. She just finished her tests and will have to have surgery in the morning. They think it might be an ectopic pregnancy … or cancer."

I hung up the phone and sat down on the couch, my eyes fixed on the little statue of Mary I kept on the desk. There was nothing I could do to stop the tears. It was a feeling that was both old and new. Old because, my family had known a lot of sickness; new, because this time it was my own mother. Ten hours later the doctors confirmed the cancer diagnosis. The following morning I gassed up the car and headed out to Iowa to see her.

When I see my mother again in heaven the first thing I will tell her is "Thank you." It's true that God gives each person a vocation from the moment of their creation, but I never could have discovered mine if it weren't for my mom. Rather, if it weren't for my moms. I guess I won't really know until I see Our Lady face-to-face how instrumental she was in bringing me to her Son.

"You Really Ought to Give Iowa a Try

"Oh, kids. Isn't this great? Or does it make you want to go to school and learn something so you don't have to spend your life on a farm?" said Dad, winking at us over his shoulder as he stuffed another sack of weeds into the truck.

My brother and sisters and I rolled our eyes at each other, but kept working. There were still acres to go. The sun baked the back of my neck and cooked my feet in my Nikes. As we walked through the rows of soybeans, we had to pull the weeds out from between the young plants. It was hard work and we kids hated it; nonetheless, there are times when I would give anything to have those long summer days back. Life in our Iowa hometown was simple. It was beautiful. But even as a girl, I knew I wasn't going to stay there forever.

My Catholic school days at Our Lady of Mt. Carmel grade school and Kuemper Catholic High School came to a close. When we were graduating, we started to joke about what we were going to do.

"If I don't get married by the time I'm thirty," I joked, "I swear I'll become a nun."

As if.

I had other plans.

My big dreams and I moved to the University of South Dakota to study Laboratory Science. South Dakota and Iowa weren't opposite worlds, but the minor culture change of being away from my family and living immersed in a public college did me good. I developed my independence, my self-confidence (I'd always been shy) and strengthened my Catholic convictions.

*S*AME *C*ORN, *N*EW *S*TATE

I studied, I graduated – and I found myself as a medical technologist in Omaha, Nebraska. Life as a young career woman seemed ideal, at least for a start. When Mom got sick, however, the order of importance I gave to things quickly fell into place. Every three weeks, she came to the city for chemotherapy. During my visits with her in the hospital, I did everything to be light-hearted and to make her laugh, especially at her own situation. I figured it was the best way to handle things, both for her sake and for mine. Things were far beyond our control. We both knew it. Whether she got better or worse did not depend on us, and there was very little we could do about it. I was scared. I wanted reassurance, a definite answer. The only consolation anyone could offer was to remind me that we were in God's hands. But for me that was an uncomfortable, frustrating and frightening place to be.

*B*IRDS OF A *f*EATHER

Looking around for a parish to call my own, I was directed to St. Leo's because it had "good music" and a softball team. It also had a prayer group that rekindled the Bible study atmosphere I had back at college. Over the Gospel, grape soda and potato chips I met my soon-to-be-best friend and roommate Laura. All it took was a few games of darts and a Marian conference for she and I to click. She had grown up in Montana and was working in Omaha at a kindergarten for deaf children. I admired her big heart and I loved her humor and realistic approach to life.

Had I not met her, I know that I never would have grown like I did in the knowledge and love of my faith. On weekends and in the evenings, we spent time praying in front of abortion clinics or going to hear Catholic speakers. We longed for something more in our lives, for a way to give to others, in short, for holiness, but where could we find it?

Growing up Catholic I was familiar with Our Lady, but I can't say that prior to this point in my life I had had a strong devotion to her. Nonetheless, I began to pray the rosary every day. My trust in Mary grew, as did an awareness that she was helping me at every moment. I knew that she was the one who was leading me to Christ and the sacraments. I could feel her motherly care for me.

The topic of "vocation" did come up between Laura and I. It was not uncommon for people, upon meeting two young women whose home was practically wallpapered with religious images, who prayed the Divine Office, and who read papal encyclicals together, to ask us: "Have you ever thought …?" I would smile and laugh self-assuredly, but would never answer. Of course

I had thought, and was thinking. Having a vocation made me nervous. I wanted to be married and have a family. I wanted to be like my mother. I was doing everything I could think of to live as a faithful Catholic. Wasn't God pleased enough with that? The faster thirty approached, I tried to forget about the joke I used to make when I was seventeen. That was just a joke. Right?

*a T*IME TO *P*ART

Alone in the hospital chapel, I buried my face in my hands and wept. Over and over I repeated the "Our Father" until I could say, "Your will be done."

God doesn't want evil things to happen and he doesn't take pleasure in human suffering. But in our walk through this valley of tears, pain is unavoidable. God's love and power aren't for the removing of suffering, but for bringing immeasurable good out of it. Mom was dying. Although we were scattered about the country, all of my siblings made it home in time to say goodbye.

As the oldest daughter, I had always confided in Mom and had been close to her. But I had never told her that I was thinking of a vocation — it was too personal, and I still wasn't sure about it. Now, as she lay silently on the hospital bed, I reached over, grabbed her hand and pressed it to my face.

"Mom," the tears almost choked me. "When you get to Heaven, you have to help me know what my vocation is. I don't know what God wants me to do."

Mustering her last ounces of strength she looked at me. I

felt her love so strongly in that moment. She was exhausted. Not just from a three-year battle with cancer, but from a lifetime of spending herself completely, serving her husband and children continuously and loving limitlessly. She said nothing, but I understood everything. She would pray for me; she would always take care of me.

The following day, Mom passed away. All any of us could say to her in her last moments were: "Thank you; I love you."

I am certain that she remembered what I had asked her before she died, for in the months following, I began to see my vocation more and more clearly. Now I had two mothers in heaven to help me follow wherever he would lead me.

REGNUM CHRISTI ENTERS THE PICTURE

Laura and I walked through the crowd to look at the booths at another Marian conference.

"Michelle, remember that group of priests we read about in the magazine last week?"

"Which? The Legion of Christ?" I asked.

"Yes, they said there's something for women. Not nuns, but consecrated, or something like that. They've got a table here."

She zigzagged her way between people, stands, and strollers to find the booth. Two consecrated women stood behind a table covered with pictures of the Pope and pamphlets advertising Regnum Christi. From the moment they said "Hi," Laura was absorbed, asking questions, and talking with them. I didn't pay much attention.

"Michelle, imagine, we can give two years of our life as volunteers! How about that?"

"Hmm… That's interesting," came my distracted reply. I left Laura there and went over to another table full of books about Marian apparitions, surreptitiously glancing at Laura who was in deep conversation with these new 'discoveries.' Was I interested?

"Lord, I'm too much of a homebody," I thought. "Who would want to leave their home for two years?"

Weeks passed by and nothing became of our brush with Regnum Christi. We both forgot about it all together, until one day an invitation to Spiritual Exercises given by a Legionary priest arrived in the mail.

*V*OCATIONAL *W*ATERS *S*TART *S*TIRRING

"Have you ever thought of a vocation?"

It was a Saturday night, two days into the spiritual exercises, and I was sitting across the desk in front of the priest. I had gone to him in need of some serious spiritual direction. He cut straight to the chase and his question was so direct that I felt like crawling under the desk out of embarrassment.

"Well not really, Father. I just want to be a faithful Catholic and get married."

Oh sure, Michelle. Who was I fooling? Father left the

question there for me to pray over in the retreat.

Shortly after the spiritual exercises had ended, Laura and I bought round trip tickets for a Holy Week retreat to be held in Rhode Island. I was not sold on the idea. It was almost a duty of conscience. Laura was the opposite. She had given our address to the consecrated women and told them that we'd love to have them visit if they were in the area. I always considered the consecrated as "Laura's visitors" but I liked their company. There was a lot that we had in common. We'd talk about the Church, the world ... and soon I discovered that I liked them. Trying to appear indifferent, I would look at them seated on the couch, and try to imagine myself as one of them.

Y_{ES}, *I H*_{AVE AN} *I*_{NKLING} ...

The Holy Week retreat at the Formation Center changed my perspective on consecrated life completely. During times of prayer, I could not muffle a voice inside of me that said: "Michelle, this might be for you."

The last talk of the evening confirmed my conviction, when one of the consecrated women said:
"If you have ever even had an inkling that you might have a vocation, you owe it to yourself and to God to find out."

I had an 'inkling' and it was impossible to continue ignoring it. I had to be faithful to what I knew Christ was saying to me in my heart. I would return to the candidacy program in July to 'find out.'

*M*ICHELLE, *M*ICHELLE, *Y*OU ARE *W*ORRIED *A*BOUT *M*ANY *T*HINGS...

Laura and I sat cross-legged on the living room floor sorting out the profits from the afternoon's garage sale.

"Don't you have this sense of freedom? I feel like St. Francis of Assisi!" Laura's "vocational joy" annoyed me. Sense of freedom? What sense did any of what I was about to do make? I was going for a two-month vocational discernment program on the other side of the country. I had resigned from my job the week before. I was now selling everything I owned. And I was going to wear a skirt all summer (a thought that made my family laugh. We all seemed to have been born wearing Levi's). Answering God's call in my conscience was beyond any sensible reasoning I could come up with.

Laura and I were together a lot during the candidacy, but we never spoke about our discernment. We didn't want to influence the other's decision. Just because one of us might stay or go, we didn't want to make the other feel that she, being the best friend, had to do the same. We gave each other the silent, spiritual support to be generous with whatever Christ would ask.

Naturally I went through moments of doubt, insecurity and temptation before the big step. I asked myself what had happened to my dreams of marriage and family. I wondered if I would really be happy, if the call I felt were real or if it were just my imagination. No one ever looked me in the eye and said, "Michelle, you have a vocation. God wants you to be consecrated." Yet even though I couldn't quite explain why, I felt secure. Inside my heart was the certainty that Christ, who had brought me thus far, would not deceive me, let me down, or leave me hanging out to dry.

It was July 29, the feast of St. Martha. I knelt in prayer before the Eucharist. Two things kept going through my mind: the first was something I heard from one of the consecrated. She had said:

"No man could ever fill a heart that was made for Christ alone." Was that why in all the men I had dated, I'd known none was meant for me?

The second idea I couldn't shake was a story one of the priests told us during the candidacy. When he was visiting the novitiate still trying to figure out if the priesthood was for him, the superior told him: "This is the third time you've been here; who are you kidding?" For me that was a wake-up call to face facts. This was the third time I had been to the Formation Center. What was I waiting for?

I prayed. And I prayed. And I prayed.

"God, give me strength. Help me to see your will. Help me to say yes to whatever you ask of me."

I listened in silence; my prayer was answered. Christ was calling me; it was clear, and the power of it flooded my soul like a wave.

Not until after Laura and I had boarded the plane to go visit our families before beginning spiritual exercises did I find out that she too had made her decision on St. Martha's feast day. It was one of those divine coincidences. Should it have been so surprising? Hadn't God been letting us be instruments of his grace for each other for the past seven years? Why should he stop now?

⌒

Moms, as I said before, play a big role in every vocation. I thank God for mine and I trust that just as they helped me to see and to accept my vocation, they will help me to be faithful to it every day for the rest of my life.

THE MEANING OF LIFE

Anne-Marie Dardis

"Let's have some wine and talk about the meaning of life!" said my friend Suzanne, clicking her ticket through the meter as we took the Metro home from work one Friday afternoon.

We were both young independent career women in Washington DC, and the meaning of life didn't mean much. The "meaning of life" was our boyfriends, the party we'd gone to last weekend, the latest gossip about someone who got stoned off the job, the clothes we'd seen in the latest Vanity Fair. But after she'd left my apartment that night, and I got ready to go out with my boyfriend to a local club, I started to think seriously, maybe for the first time:

What is the meaning of my life? This… ?

I decided to worry about how I should fix my lipstick.

"CRADLE CATHOLIC"

If I'd looked back at my Catholic childhood in the South, I might have had an answer to that question. As it was, I was too busy trying to get rid of my Southern accent and being a hit in the

Metropolis. Something other than a cocktail had to shake me up.

I can never separate my childhood from my Catholic faith. Every night my nine brothers and sisters, my parents and I would assemble at my parents' bedside to pray the rosary in front of my mother's collection of Madonnas. New Orleans, where I grew up, might have a "party-town" reputation, but it is steeped in Catholic culture. Our Good Friday Bike Pilgrimages were a good example. Dad invented them to give us something spiritual to do on the most solemn day of the year, and carrying on an old Catholic tradition of accompanying Christ in his agony by visiting nine churches. Once inside, we'd follow Mom and Dad up to the front, and kneel down to pray beside them. I remember kneeling beside them when I was six or seven, and thinking: 'why is that man there on the cross?' I knew it was Jesus. I knew he had died for me. I just didn't understand why he was there.

By the time I entered high school, I thought I'd found a little of the meaning of life. I had earned the tag "Julie McCoy," thanks to the entertainment coordinator who starred on The Loveboat. Planning the weekend, planning proms and planning VIP parties for visiting diplomats was my forte. When it came time to depart from the high school scene, "my plans" raised their head high. I'd breeze through college and then have a great big family with eight kids and a loving husband — every girl's dream, at least every Catholic girl's dream. And I was sure it would come true.

I took the first step. 'Viva Kappa Kappa Gamma' life could have been my motto in my freshman and junior years at Louisiana State University. I loved the parties, the football games, and the fraternity boys. It was one night, really late as I was cleaning up after a party with a couple of my friends who were still more or less sober, that I realized it wasn't enough. Maybe I needed something more. A new university?

I switched my major to Communications at Loyola University, with an internship at the New Orleans Tourist Commission … and all of a sudden, I was in my graduation gown, with the mortarboard in hand, clutching my diploma. What was the next step? Those two years at Loyola had flown by in a busy social whirl. I gasped for breath at the end of it to think about what came next.

"Anne-Marie, you could be doing anything with your life. Anything," a friend assured me at a party.

I didn't want just anything. I wanted my plans: success, marriage, and a big family.

The success part came first. I landed a job in advertising and PR at a good hotel in New Orleans. I moved out of my house. I had everything I wanted. Almost. Marriage and the big family still seemed to be a little vague. My most likely future husband prospect was making plans for graduate school, which pushed my plans into an uncertain future. That white wedding gown I'd seen at the boutique might have to wait a couple of years.

Into the fast Lane

But soon it seemed my life was taking a new direction. I started dating Christopher, the gorgeous guy who worked with me at the hotel, and then I decided to move to Washington DC.

I had friends there, and he was attending law school nearby. Plus, I landed an incredible job with the NASDAQ Stock Market, doing event planning and marketing – my specialty. I was on my way! Or so I thought.

I drove into D.C. and immediately signaled into the fast lane. An impressive job, with travel opportunities, happy hours, clubbing and cocktail parties — everything I'd wanted. My boyfriend and I were a perfect match: he was going to be a famous lawyer, and I was going to be a famous PR expert. I had the right friends, the right boyfriend, the right job and the right clothes. I ought to have everything I wanted. But I didn't. Maybe New Orleans Society Life was a bit different from the East Coast, but Washington DC made me sick. I did most of my thinking at night, after the parties, trying to push aside the images I'd had to face, and sometimes having the betraying thought:

'Anne-Marie. Is it really worth it? Is this what you really want?' And then I'd push the thought aside. 'Oh shut up. I have all the "right" things. It's my problem I'm not satisfied with them yet.'

But was success worth everything I thought it was? And more importantly, was it the meaning of life I was looking for?

Work was a moral minefield. My colleagues were getting fired: one for sexual harassment, another for embezzling money. Or else they spent their lives in the office trying to get ahead, while their families were left at home alone. Some never even thought of having a family because they were so wrapped up in climbing the corporate ladder. Would Christopher and I end up like that?

I finally had to admit to myself that above and beyond my dreams to have a corner office, was my desire to raise a family, just as my parents had. I somehow sensed that being the greatest career woman and most elegant social butterfly was not going to get me all the way there.

I just never thought about it long enough to do something about it.

RING RING ...

"Hello," I said, as I picked up the phone.
"Is this Anne-Marie?" a strange male voice asked.
"Yes, it is ..."

Mom. She already knew that I had a boyfriend, but that didn't deter her from giving out my phone number to the "eligible" [definition: Catholic. Young. Reasonably intelligent.] men she came across.

"Look," I tried to say kindly, "I think I might be busy ..."

There was no escape. I was almost forced into meeting him. He turned out to be nice enough, though, and I didn't have to meet him alone. We had dinner with his sister, her family and another of my sisters. It was his sister who opened the door for me as we were leaving to tell me:
"By the way, there's a group of young people in the area

who offer a way to get to know and to strengthen you in the faith. Here's the phone number if you're interested. Why don't you go?"

"OK, " I shrugged. It sounded all right.

I sat down at the back of the room and opened my purse for my compact mirror.

"How long do we have to stay?" hissed Suzanne.

"If it's boring, we're leaving," I said, folding up the mirror.

We were surrounded by other young people chatting, laughing and waiting for the Legionary priest who was going to present a talk on Making Christ the Center of Your Lent, organized by a group of young people in Regnum Christi.

"Anne-Marie! How are you?" asked Carolyn, the sister of the nice enough guy.

"Fine," I said.

"I have to tell you –"

But she didn't get a chance to finish because the priest entered to begin his talk. I'd expected to be bored. I wasn't. He was funny, and some of the things he said blew dust off my Catholic faith. It was even a little uncomfortable, because I wasn't sure I wanted to be reminded about them … and I didn't hang around afterwards. Suzanne and I got in my car to go back. I turned on the engine to warm up the car on the chilly March night.

"Anne-Marie, you do the weirdest things sometimes," said Suzanne, pulling on her seatbelt. "Didn't Christopher ask you out tonight?"

"It's not like he really asks me any more. He expects me to

go with him. It's like: Anne-Marie-I'm-going-to-Jerry's-see-you-there kind of invitation."
Suzanne made a face.
"Typical."
I shrugged, and backed out of the parking lot.

The next day, although Suzanne and I laughed at work about the meeting, the half-sunk truths of childhood faith wouldn't re-submerge themselves. They floated up at the strangest times and I found myself wanting to know more, somehow. Plus, I was discovering that Christopher and I weren't the most perfect couple …

What a coincidence. Another Regnum Christi activity was the first thing that crossed my path.

I entered a conference room full of young professionals, only to find the same priest leading the talk. This time, I was by myself – I had no excuses to leave early. When the talk was over, I stayed around at the back, talking to the others there.
"So," said a young woman my age passing me a cup of coffee and offering me a tray of cookies. "Where are you working?"

We started talking. They were like me: successful, hardworking – but there was something different. They wanted to do something more with their time than work and socialize. They'd say how they were trying to change their workplace, what they were doing to help the Church – it seemed almost unbelievable. I'd never thought that the faith that I'd grown up with was lived anywhere outside my family. I decided to go to a Regnum Christi retreat that Leah, the one I'd first started talking to, mentioned.

"Hi, Anne-Marie?" said another unfamiliar voice over the phone, a couple of days later. This time it was a woman.

"Hello?" I said, twisting my pen cap off so that I could write down the things I needed to buy to survive that week. Coffee was first on the list. I was out. And if this was another door-to-door saleswoman ...

"This is Leah. Do you remember me?"

It took a minute –

"Oh, oh, hi! How are you?"

"Great! I just wanted to let you know about the retreat. It's going to be at a retreat center about an hour from here. Oh, and did I tell you that it's in silence?"

"For two days?"

"It's great, Anne-Marie. You're going to love it. Just you and God."

Oh. Yeah - great.

*W*HAT *I* *R*EALLY *M*EAN *I*S ...

I knelt down in the chapel, during one of the breaks that we had, and put my head in my hands. I felt like everything was pouring on me at once, all the things I'd never realized, all the time I'd spent just for myself :

"Lord, I'm so sorry ..."

The crucifix and the tabernacle looked on me in serene silence as I knelt there, crying. In front of the crucifix, looking at the statue of a dead man covered with wounds, bleeding from a crown of thorns and in front of the tabernacle where the real Christ was waiting, silently, constantly, for me – it was impossible for me not to face up to my reality.

"You loved me so much …" and I had loved myself so much. The meaning of my life wasn't me. In that still chapel I saw that there was more to life than cocktail parties, Revlon lipstick and sitting in coffee shops with my friends. I'd heard it from my parents, but finally, I understood. I thought over the retreat: directed meditations on all Christ had done for me, the prayer and silence, the reception of the sacraments, the whole environment of the retreat – and I realized that I needed some advice. There was this thing being offered called spiritual direction. I wasn't sure what it was, but it sounded like something I needed.

The priest and I talked for a while, maybe half an hour. He asked me about my situation, my relationship with God, and I found myself telling him all of what had been happening in my life, what I was looking for … He didn't get shocked by what I told him. He didn't give me a hell-and-brimstone sermon. He listened, patiently, and gave me advice that seemed to fit perfectly. And then, at the end, he said:

"Anne-Marie, have you ever thought of becoming a member of Regnum Christi?"

That was the last thing I thought he'd ask me to do. I thought of the retreat I'd had; the people I knew in Regnum

Christi, the bits and pieces that I'd been able to read of the writing of their founder, Fr. Marcial Maciel, LC.

"I'd never heard of it before, Father; but what it teaches is what my parents have always tried to raise me with. I'd just never seen it anyplace else but here."

"I think you should consider becoming a member. It's going to help you after this retreat."

Should I take the step of commitment to Christ and Regnum Christi? It would mean drastic changes to my party lifestyle; it would require putting Christ first, and not myself; it would mean accountability for my life before God. Was I ready for it? I knew, though, that this was something God wanted, and if I really wanted peace and happiness in my life, I should follow him.

I decided to incorporate into Regnum Christi, to take my faith seriously and to begin building a deeper relationship with God. He had put Regnum Christi in my path to help me do just that.

*T*HE *N*EW *I*MPROVED *a*NNE-*M*ARIE

It was Friday night. I was getting ready in front of the mirror in my bedroom as usual, but this time it wasn't for a happy hour with Christopher.

I was working in Regnum Christi with all my planning might. Parties with guest speakers talking about Catholic issues had become a bit more of a priority than happy hours. And then, Christopher and I had broken up. We just didn't have the same interests anymore. I didn't want a life full of garages of Jaguars and weekends to the Caribbean – that wasn't going to fulfill me. That wasn't the meaning of my life. I wanted a real family, where I could bring the faith to my children. I was putting all my talents into Regnum Christi's events, but I didn't stop there. I wanted to know my Faith – and to know Christ better.

I began saying morning prayers, attending Mass more frequently, going to Gospel reflections and Eucharistic hours, and having regular spiritual direction, all of which Regnum Christi offered. Then, Saturday mornings became tennis lessons. Sunday mornings were catechism classes for first graders. I'm not sure who learned more, the first graders or myself. Every Sunday morning, I would find myself in front of a wiggling group of six and seven year-olds, eyes wide and eager, with hands ready to wave in the air and tell me:

"Miss Anne-Marie but what if …"

"If God is like that what if …"

As I cleaned up the classroom, sometimes, I would think about how I used to spend Sunday mornings. Or how, if Christopher had seen me, he'd think I was crazy.

I didn't regret it. Each one of the children I taught was so absolutely different, so individual that I realized that God loves each of us. And he doesn't love us and leave us – he has a plan for each of us. That's why he made us so differently. Maybe he was planning that Robert, the slightly chubby boy in the front row would be an engineer; and Molly, with her long blonde hair and her preference for drawing in the margins might become a famous illustrator. Alex was going to be a doctor, maybe. And I could see the mothers and the fathers, and the Catholic families they might have in the future ... I thought about how special each one of them was. I thought about how God loved each one of them; and I started to think of the plan that perhaps he would have for me. Because when I looked at them and thought of who they might be, I also saw the other range of possibilities: drug users, another statistic on the suicide role, another teen pregnancy, unhappy divorcees ...

I needed to do more.

I began to feel restless in my job at NASDAQ. It didn't fit anymore. It wasn't that it was bad, but I wasn't fulfilled doing it. I knew that I needed to do something besides it.

"God, what do you want from me?" I found myself asking.

These questions bothered me until one day, in spiritual direction, I found an unexpected and surprising answer.

"Are you fighting against a vocation?"

"No, I am NOT," I declared, defensively, "I'm going to get married and have children."

How many times had I told my spiritual director that? Of course I didn't have a vocation to get consecrated. I wanted to get married.

"Okay, I was just asking," he replied.

Driving home afterwards, I began to think more about it. Why did I fly off the handle at such an innocent question? Of course I was going to have a great husband and lots of kids. But, what if I do have a vocation?

I unlocked the door of my apartment and looked around. It seemed like there was a question hanging all the way across the room. 'Anne-Marie,' I thought, 'you really have to face this one. Okay. Okay.' I took a breath. If – if - I had a vocation, God would have to tell me. Standing in my apartment, I said out loud:
"Okay Lord. I'm going to say my rosary every day, and you'd better tell me ..."

As good as my intentions were, I didn't hold up my end of the bargain for very long. Holy Week arrived and I was still in the dark.

"God, please, please, please tell me what you want me to do. I can't keep living without knowing."
The big wooden crucifix hung above the altar and as I knelt before the image of Christ that Holy Thursday, I begged him for an answer. God has his timing; he knows the moment we are ready to hear what he has to tell us, and for me, this was not it. I didn't get any of the specifics, I left the church with a peaceful sense that he had something BIG planned for my life, that it would be wonderful and the he would show it to me soon.

a foretaste of the Rest of My Life

"Anne- Marie!" squealed Claire, standing in front of my desk at work and looking down at the assortment of Bible, Styrofoam coffee cups, papers, compact, comb and computer strewn around me. "But you can't leave this weekend. Did you hear about the party at the deLuses'?"

I shrugged.

I was going to St. Louis for a Regnum Christi women's convention.

Getting off the plane, I found my way to the hotel where we were staying.

"Hi, Anne-Marie," said a smiling woman in a skirt with a wedding ring on her finger and a face that almost shone. She radiated joy. "My name is Elisabeth. I'm helping with the convention this weekend, so if you need anything, just let me know."

As she helped me get my bags to my room, she told me that she was a consecrated woman in Regnum Christi. She'd given her life to serve Christ and the Church, she said. I think that the consecrated women were the ones I remember most from that weekend. They were so – different, not weird different, real and different at the same time. During a conference given by one of the consecrated, the wheels started turning as she quoted the Gospel passage about the talents:

> "I tell you to everyone who has, more will be given, but from the one who has not, even what he has will be taken away" (Luke 19:26).

God entrusts everyone with gifts and talents, I knew that, but standing at the podium was a woman who had placed every single one of those talents at God's service. Perhaps I should give more to Christ, as they had. The perhaps became more and more pronounced as the convention went on.

I casually cornered one of the consecrated women and tried to look nonchalant.

"So," I said. And I began spilling out the most vocationally oriented questions: What is your prayer life like? What apostolates do you do? How do you know if God is calling you?

She answered my questions as though they were the most normal things anyone might want to know. As she got up, I breathed a sigh of relief. She hadn't guessed, so I thought. I'm sure she must have been laughing to herself inside. I was practically wearing a "V" for vocation on my forehead!

It stayed in my mind. Belonging totally to Christ in heart, mind and body, spending myself to bring Christ to others, to defend the Church, to rebuild the family and society ... they were my feelings and my desires. Was God asking me? I was supposed to work on planning an event on the plane ride home, but I could hardly concentrate on the numbers and the invitations. Perhaps it wasn't a coincidence. I knew it wasn't.

I decided to spend the summer discerning in their candidacy program.

TOTAL SURRENDER

What I experienced during the candidacy is hard to put into words. I was there to figure out what Christ wanted of me, that much I had clear. I had classes together with the other candidates, we enjoyed each other's friendship, but above all, day after day, I spent long periods of time speaking with Christ in the Blessed Sacrament. This is where I discovered my vocation. I met Christ, a living Christ, a person. And that Christ is God, my Creator, the one who had my life planned out from the beginning of time, the one who more than anyone else on this planet loved me and wanted me to be happy. I couldn't help but falling in love with him.

'Anne-Marie,' I realized one day, 'this is the meaning of your life. It's God. And he wants your whole life'.

*B*REAKING THE *N*EWS

How did my family react? Well, needless to say, they were a little shocked. Of all my siblings, I was the last one that anyone had imagined to have a vocation. But, they saw how happy I was and knew that God's hand had been directing my life. I was very sure about my decision and this assured them as well.

My friends and colleagues thought I was crazy.
"Rather than doing something rash, why don't you take a six-month sabbatical to go and figure out your life?" my boss asked me.
"That's what I've been doing, but in six weeks!" I responded assuredly.

Deep inside, I felt an immense peace, difficult to put into

words. I told my friends that it seemed like I had been sucked into a magnetic field, but with absolutely no desire to escape. It was bittersweet; I was both happy and sad, but I knew that I was about to do something very exciting.

*a W*HOLE *N*EW *W*ORLD

It was difficult to stop making my own plans and no longer having my credit cards, car, closet full of clothes, snow skis and the freedom of doing, going and having what I wanted whenever I wanted.

But then what were snow skis compared to eternal bliss?

All of my struggles were overcome by the deep fulfillment I had found in Christ. Every day is new, different, something more, because every day has the one meaning that I was made for – Christ.

⁐

Some days, I find myself stepping into the chapel, to make a quick visit and saying:
"Hello, again. Did you know that you're the meaning of my life?"

To Heal a Suffering Humanity

Caroline Wilders

*O*ur family had rushed last minute into a middle pew at church and I was squeezed between my little brother and sister, contemplating the broken arm held across my chest in a sling. It was the result of tumbling from a magnolia tree a few weeks before.

My brother pinched me.

"Stop it," I snapped, and elbowed him with my good arm. Mum turned to glare at both of us. I picked up my chin and determinedly tried to look virtuous as I listened to the priest read the Gospel. All of a sudden, a phrase jumped out at me.

"What I tell you in the dark, utter in the light; and what you hear whispered, proclaim upon the housetops."
(Matthew 10:27)

Me?

I was not a graceful child and I was extremely shy, so the

thought of having to shout to thousands of people while perched on a rooftop without falling seemed impossible. There had to be a better way to love Jesus, a way in which I could speak to people about him one at a time, with two feet on the ground. That's when I decided to become a doctor.

The decision matured in my heart and soul. I dreamed of going to Africa or the Amazon to be a missionary doctor. I wanted my life to help others and to bring them close to God, especially those most needy.

This was God's way of planting the seed that blossomed into my decision to consecrate my life to him completely.

A Tale of Two Cities

Grave's End, despite the morbid name, was not a bad place to grow up. It was right by the Thames River, a little outside of London, England. There were plenty of children to play with besides my little brothers and sister. I happily spent the first fourteen years of my life there. There and in France - my father is English and my mother is French, so I spent my childhood with my winters in England and my summer holidays crossing the Channel to visit my mum's family in Southern France.

Mum was determined that her children would be perfectly bilingual. We only spoke French at home, and homework had to be done twice - once in English for the teacher and again in French for Mum. During the summer, when school should have been over, there was no escape from Mum's intensive French grammar classes.

*L*IFESTYLES OF THE *P*LAIN AND *S*IMPLE

Besides the two nationalities, two languages, and two cultures, by far, the greatest gift my parents passed on to their children was the one Catholic faith. Mum and Dad sought always to give us the best religious formation and to raise us in the best possible surroundings for our faith to grow and mature. In part, this was what motivated them to move the family from England to Monaco when I was fourteen.

Monaco is known to the world as the "Home of the Rich and Famous," a tax haven located on the sunny shores of the Mediterranean, on the Côte d'Azur (very glamorous…), but the majority of those who live there are normal everyday people.

My family certainly fell into this category. We lived in two apartments side by side, because we couldn't afford a house. To avoid confusion and to make life simpler, we kept the keys permanently in the doors. At one point in time there were seventeen burglaries on our street, but it must have been obvious that there was nothing worth taking at our house because even with the keys in the doors, no one ever robbed us.

The move was difficult at first. Every dislocation from familiar surroundings always is; and it was hard to leave my school and my friends. I understood why we had to move, but it didn't make it any easier.

The morning I walked into my new classroom, a sick feeling spread in my stomach. I looked at my new school mates, sitting in rows of straight desks with their faces turned inquistively to me. I knew no one. They had all known each other since kindergarten. Even with my perfect French, everyone knew I was British, which didn't make fitting in any easier. I had long since overcome my childhood shyness, but this new situation made me become less outgoing and sure of myself. Since my social life was not thriving, I spent a great deal of my time studying and tutoring struggling students. In the end, this gave me the chance to make new friends and "prove myself" to my classmates.

Worse than this, Monaco didn't have the Catholic environment my parents expected. They hoped to be part of a society where Catholicism was the norm, not the exception. Yet though there were more Catholic churches, my parents, brothers, sister and I were almost the only non-gray haired people in them. Out of the 120 students at my school, only five were practicing Catholics.

I see now that this was part of God's divine Providence for my family and the beginning of a new stage in his plan over me. Cut off from external securities and distractions, God's presence in my life became more and more real. He showed me that he was the only truly faithful and reliable friend, and I could seek consolation and companionship only in him.

To Christ Through Mary

Time passed, but my dream to become a doctor didn't. I

entered a high school especially focused on math and science to prepare myself for entrance into medical school.

One Saturday morning at the breakfast table when I was sixteen my mother put down the coffee pot, looked at me and said:

"Caroline, have you ever thought about volunteering in Lourdes for the summer? Madame Brun was telling me the other day that her son Marc went there last summer to help with the sick pilgrims."

My father looked up from his newspaper.

"Might be good if you want to be a doctor, Caroline."

Lourdes?

The choice between being able to spend my summer helping others or sticking out a lonely two months between two apartments in Monaco wasn't difficult. I remembered, too, the stories my mother had told us as we were growing up of the appearance of the Blessed Virgin Mary to Bernadette Soubirous. At the grotto in Lourdes, Bernadette was instructed by Our Lady to dig in the ground and to wash in the water. As she scratched at the earth with her fingers, muddy water sprang up. She began smearing the mud on her arms and face as the onlookers stared at her as though she'd lost her senses. Little did they know that in a matter of hours that mud puddle would turn into a vibrant spring, turning out over 32,000 gallons of water per day. Many sick and handicapped people have since been miraculously cured by bathing or washing in this spring; sixty-nine miracles have been approved officially by the Catholic Church, but many others consider themselves cured even if their case has not been declared a miracle. Doctors, nurses, and volunteers are always needed in Lourdes to look after and care for these pilgrims.

Mum's suggestion was all I needed. Although the official age for volunteering was eighteen, I was so eager to go that I asked for and obtained a special exception. I spent that summer (and the five following) in Lourdes preparing meals, making beds, assisting the nurses, escorting the pilgrims and praying to Our Lady to point out the proper jungle for me to carry out my missionary work as a doctor. By the end of the summer, I was thoroughly exhausted, yet eager to return. From the five summers I spent at Lourdes as a volunteer, there are hundreds of beautiful stories I could tell; however, one episode in particular is worth mentioning.

Substantial Humility

It was towards the end of my first summer as a volunteer.

"Bless me, Father, for I have sinned…"

The bearded Benedictine on the other side of the confessional sat quietly as I unloaded my woes. I cried as I told him how reluctant I was to return to school. After listening to all I had to say, the monk turned toward me, looked me in the eyes and asked:

"Are you willing to do whatever penance I give you?"
"Of course, Father."
I never knew one had a choice in these matters.

"Good," he replied. "Then I want you to go to the grotto of Our Lady, lie face down on the ground before her image and, there, in prayer for 20 minutes, I want you to give your life to her completely."

Oh my.

"That's really my penance?"

"Yes; and I absolve you from your sins…"

What had I just committed myself to? I left the confessional stunned, my ears already hot with embarrassment at the mere thought of what I was about to do.

Thinking I had to do the penance that same day, I waited until the last possible moment. The later it was, I thought, the fewer people would see me – or worse – to step on me. The minutes crept by. 11 p.m. — too many people. 11:30 p.m. — still too many people. Why wouldn't they all just go to bed already? 11:40 p.m. — this was it, now or never. My heart thumped and my legs shook. Here you go, Our Lady, I prayed as I got on my knees and lay down on my stomach.

"Are you alright?" someone said, rushing over and shaking my arm.

"Yes, I'm fine. Thank you," I mumbled into the ground.

The gravel pressed into my face. I was saturated with embarrassment. This was ridiculous; what was I doing? As I debated with myself about whether or not to get up and leave, a thought crossed my mind:

"Caroline, you're here now. Everyone's seen you already. Put your life in your mother's hands."

I began to pray, simply, to tell Our Lady all I had in my heart: school, my desire to be a doctor, my family's situation, my friends (and lack of them). I confided in her my desires to be able to do something — anything to help others and to serve God; my search for the right jungle to go to, and I found there was no reason to dread going back to Monaco. Mary was taking care of me.

The bell rang; the grotto was about to close.

I pulled myself up from where I had been, taking a last look at my mother's image shining in the grotto where she had appeared to Bernadette such a long time ago. A little group of bystanders watched me curiously as I escaped, avoiding their eyes and hurrying off back to the hotel.

I had done something for God, which under no circumstances I would have done for myself. It forced me to overcome the fear of what other people would say and think, freeing me to live facing God, concerned only about his opinion. This same authenticity and loyalty would be asked of me on many more occasions in years to come, in my training to be a doctor and in the everyday living of my consecrated life. Of course, I didn't know that – but I knew something was different. From then on I made a point to go back to confession with this same Benedictine monk every year when I was in Lourdes.

LEAST LIKELY TO SUCCEED

With the passing of time, I adapted to life in Monaco. I

found a circle of close friends, and going to school ceased to be a dreaded event. In my last year of high school, however, I did the unbelievable.

After having focused intensely on math and science, and only on math and science, for three straight years, I swopped my studies to languages and philosophy.

"But you're ruining your chances of getting into medical school," my friends protested.

I didn't care. When my professor assigned a three-page paper proving that two plus two really did equal four I decided I'd had enough. If it were truly my vocation to be a doctor, God would find the way, because I couldn't put up with such nonsense another minute.

Despite the verdict that my year would be an academic death sentence, I enjoyed every minute of it. The autumn afterwards, I began classes in the medical school of the University of Nice, near home, but in France. That wasn't such an achievement. In France, anyone who has graduated from high school having passed the tough final exam, the baccalaureate, can enter medical school; the trick is staying in.

*M*EDICINE *101*

Medical school in France works like this: anyone with a baccalaureate can enroll, but only 100 will pass the first year. Regardless of talent, regardless of class size — only the top 100. Any student who doesn't make the cut the first time around has one chance to repeat the year. If, after that second try, he still doesn't make it into the top 100, he's lost all chance of ever getting into a medical school anywhere in France.

My freshman class had 800 students. Eight hundred competing for the top 100 places. It was every student for himself. Students caring only about securing their place did so by any means. They ripped pages out of textbooks so that no one else would have access to needed information, they sold cheat sheets with incorrect answers, and they "gently persuaded" other students to drop out.

I was lucky enough to be in medical school with two very good friends. The three of us studied together, stood up for each other and stuck together no matter what. At the end of that first year, all three of us had made the top 100.

However, even with that hurdle cleared, the road to the rest of my medical career was far from smooth. My friends and I confronted principles and practices contrary to our ethics and values.

This was the moment, God thought, that Regnum Christi would cross my path.

FR. PIERRE

I opened the door to Fr. Pierre, who stepped inside with a

big smile and greeted me, saying:

"You must be Caroline."

"Come in," I said.

We'd heard that my mother's second cousin's wife's cousin had recently been ordained a priest in the diocese of Monaco. My parents sought him out and invited him over for dinner.

My father was waiting in the living room. He offered Fr.Pierre a glass of wine and they began to make conversation with the awkwardness of new acquaintances. Fr. Pierre was originally from Paris and had become a member of something called Regnum Christi before his ordination. Now he was carrying out his priestly ministry in Monaco and working to start the Movement in Monaco and France.

We sat down at the dinner table and Fr. Pierre asked me what I was doing.

"Me? I'm in medical school, in my second year in Nice," I said.

"Oh," he nodded. "How are things going?"

"Fine," I shrugged.

I hadn't told my parents about the struggles I was having in medical school because I didn't want them to get nervous, and besides, I supposed that it was part of the process every medical student simply had to endure in order to become a doctor.

Later that evening, as Fr. Pierre was pulling his coat back on and saying goodbye to all of us, he mentioned to me:

"If you get your friends together I can give you courses on medical ethics. It might help, Caroline. It's not easy being a doctor."

He was right. I needed to know more about what I was doing. It wasn't enough just to have a funny feeling that something didn't quite fit between my faith and my training; I needed to know what was right and wrong. And I didn't.

A week later, five of my medical schoolmates and I were sitting in my living room hanging on to Fr. Pierre's every word. Even though he was only giving us the basic principles of the Church's teaching on life issues, after two years of studying and working in such a callous and ethically ambiguous environment, his words seemed like a revelation.

Bioethics wasn't all Fr. Pierre taught. He told us about the Regnum Christi Movement, its mission and spirituality, and what a great idea it would be for us to start off the first Regnum Christi team in Monaco.

'Great,' I thought to myself, 'It's a shame that I don't have the time.' I lived to study. What if, because I hadn't memorized absolutely everything, a case came up I didn't know how to treat and I ended up killing my patient?

*J*ust *W*hat *I N*eeded

However, after much motivation, Fr. Pierre convinced me and two of my friends to attend a Regnum Christi young women's convention that summer near Barcelona, Spain. The convention, we were told, was to be international. Thinking that that meant "English", I calmly assured my friends:

"Don't worry, I'll translate."

The whole convention was given in Spanish and almost all the girls attending were Spanish speakers.

What did we do? My friends and I should have felt miserable and lost in this Spanish-immersed situation, but we didn't. Miraculously we were able to understand, to a greater or lesser degree, all of the talks and conferences given.

But more than the conferences, it was the other young women at the convention who convinced me of the reality of Regnum Christi. Fr. Pierre had tried to tell me anout it, but I had to see it for myself and I saw it in the other girls there. They were normal; they talked, laughed, danced, played the guitar, listened to the same music as me, and had a million practical jokes, but they were the same ones who, when I happened to go into the chapel, I would see in the pews, kneeling and talking to Christ in the tabernacle. I'd hoped for friends like them. Not only did they share my same faith and values, but by their simple way of being who they were — normal young people — they transmitted Christ to those around them.

During that convention, I met the consecrated women for the first time. I was amazed by them. They had given up everything to bring souls to Christ, to feed the spiritually hungry and to nurse the spiritually sick. They had given up everything for the sake of people like me. I felt a strong sense of admiration and gratitude toward them, though I can't say that I necessarily thought in that moment that God was calling me to do the same. I was sure I was going to be a doctor.

A Peek at the Hidden Treasure

The day before the convention ended, the chaplain gave us a retreat based on the parable of the Treasure in a Field.

"The Kingdom of Heaven is like a treasure buried in a field, which a person finds and hides again, and out of joy goes and sells all that he has and buys that field." (Matthew 13: 44-45).

Selling everything to gain God's treasure. I didn't understand very much of the talk (it was in Spanish...), but I focused on the passage. A treasure. What kind of treasure was God offering me? What did I need to sell? My studies? I put that one aside right away. God wouldn't ask me to sell my studies – I was going to be his doctor in the jungles. My rock collection? God didn't want that – neither did I, really. It was just another thing to dust in my room. Nothing seemed to really answer the question. I asked God to show me what the treasure was he was offering me – and what I needed to sell to gain it. At the end of the day, I solved the problem: the hidden treasure was the hidden qualities of each person I would meet as a doctor. The parable, it seemed, was trying to tell me to love Christ in my neighbor. Good.

But I still wasn't quite satisfied.

I was sad to leave.

"It was like a chance to breathe," I told my friends on the train home. "And now – back to medical school."

The three of us looked at each other.

"What did you think of the retreat?" I asked them.

"Fine," said Jeanne. "Not that I understood that much."

"But that passage. You know. About the treasure in the field, what did you think it was?"

"The Kingdom of Heaven," said Annette, shrugging. "That's what it says."

It did say that. But what did that mean?

*E*UREKA!

Weeks later, that same summer, I was where I always was during the summer: Lourdes. It was my twenty-first birthday. The noonday sun beat down upon the crowd of pilgrims gathered for Mass in the grotto. I, in my blue and white volunteer's apron, poured water for the sick. That particular day I was assisting a blind woman, describing the scene of thousands of pilgrims and hundreds of wheelchairs to her.

It was an international Mass, said in various languages: French, Polish, Italian, etc. As the priest stood up to read the Gospel, I set down my water pitcher to pay attention.

"The Kingdom of Heaven is like a treasure buried in a field..." First in French, then in English, then in German (the language I had learned in school), then in Spanish (the language I had picked up during the summer).

Someone should have taken the water pitcher and poured it over my head. It was all so clear! Of course! Listening to those readings of the Gospel was like God shouting at me from heaven: "Knock knock, Caroline! I am that hidden treasure. And, knock knock, to sell everything means to come follow me. And, knock knock, if you didn't catch on at first, let me repeat myself in a language you will understand!"

There I was. I had been going to Lourdes for the past five years begging Our Lady to show me where God wanted me to go. In minutes I had the answer to what God wanted of me for the rest of my life. Once I "came to" and the Mass was over, I had to take the blind lady back to her room, but the walk from the grotto to her hotel seemed to take forever. I just wanted to go to the chapel and pray, to be alone with Christ, to talk with him about all this. When that moment came and I was on my knees before him, in a state of elation, disbelief, and spiritual euphoria, I thanked him with all my heart for the greatest birthday present he could ever have given me.

All in God's Time

Now that the question of "what" God wanted of me had been answered, I still had the question of "when?"

I knew the consecrated women had their formation center in Rome, where they would dedicate the first years of their consecrated life to preparing themselves for their future apostolic work.

Did God want me to go there right away to begin consecrated life? I still had one year left of medical school. Should I go on to finish it, become a doctor, and then consecrate myself to him? What was his will?

I left Lourdes without a clear answer, but decided to leave this dilemma in God's hands, trusting that he would show me in his time and at the proper moment.

Returning home, I resumed my medical studies. It was my fourth year, so, as is the custom, I began interning at a hospital. How well God had his plan worked out for me. While I felt I was hanging in suspense about my vocation, it was precisely through my work in the hospital that God showed me his will. The dramatic cases and the suffering patients made me confront the reality of the world: people were suffering and dying for a lack of Christ, a lack for which no medical care, technology or prescription could ever compensate. The world could not wait longer; it needed him now.

I had dreamed of being a doctor since I was five, of going to the farthest reaches of the earth, to where God's love and care were most needed. A doctor's hands are like those of the Divine Physician, who soothes pain, heals wounds and alleviates suffering. The possibility of becoming a doctor was one I would have to give up forever.

"*A*ND *S*EEING THE *D*ISCIPLE *W*HOM *H*E *L*OVED…"

I'm sure it sounds ridiculous or illogical to many, and perhaps, looking from a purely natural perspective, it is, but I couldn't wait. God was calling me. I had been touched by Christ's love and could no longer resist the gentle voice beckoning me to himself.

On December 27, the feast of St. John the Evangelist, with less than one year of medical school left, I made my decision to leave everything and consecrate my life to Christ. St. John, the youngest of the apostles, didn't leave Christ suffering alone on the cross while he earned his degree. Neither would I.

Was this a difficult decision? Yes and no. Yes, for all the reasons you can easily imagine. No, because I knew clearly that this was what God wanted. Christ didn't want a medical license, he wanted me, and the only thing I wanted was him. After seventeen years of consecrated life, this hasn't changed. These have been the happiest seventeen years of my life.

~

I have worked in several countries with people of all ages and in all circumstances: those in the pits of sin, and those at the heights of holiness; those who live in material abundance and those whose sole occupation is survival. Jesus Christ is my life and my everything.

Being consecrated means being a missionary doctor in the fullest and most sublime sense of the word. My jungle is the world. My patients are anyone who needs to discover meaning in life. My prescription: Jesus Christ — take daily, fully refillable, no risk of overdose.

*M*Y *R*EAL *N*AME

Magdalena Fainé

*M*y computer is giving me a blank look. It's Saturday evening, and I've been staring out my window harvesting memories for a while now trying to think of where, or how, to begin my vocation story. But enough thinking. I'd better start to write.

In hindsight, everything that led up to the discovery of my vocation seems so obvious, but at the time, it wasn't that clear at all. Looking back over the years, God seems to point out to me all the coincidences and clues he was dropping and which I never seemed to pick up on. "Magdalena," he seems to tell me, "do you see this? And this? Remember that? That was me."

One such hint makes me laugh now. I think it was the first time I ever considered being a nun. I was lying on the living room rug watching 'The Song of Bernadette'. If nuns got to see Our Lady, then that was a good enough reason to become one. However, after having watched the way St. Bernadette had to suffer, the notion of a vocation was dismissed before the credits even began to roll.

*N*OW *I L*AY *M*E *D*OWN *T*O *S*LEEP...

"Mom," I called down the hallway.

"Go to sleep, Maida."

I lay in my bed thinking little eight year old thoughts.

I didn't like my nickname. I wondered why they had to call me Maida when my real name was Magdalena. It sounded much more elegant. But then Sister Anita's real name was Carola. They just had to call her a different name when she became a nun. If I became a nun, I would be called Sister Magdalena; because I was sure that God called me by my real name.

And when he called me, he did.

Aside from the Bernadette experience, the thought of becoming a nun never struck me. A Spanish congregation of nuns, the Handmaids of the Sacred Heart ran my school in Santiago, Chile, where I grew up, and I loved them. I always went to talk to the nuns. The sisters even came to my house for lunch, but as much as I admired and enjoyed being with them, I was the only one who seemed to overlook the obvious. Everyone thought that I had a vocation but me. After getting consecrated my parents admitted that since I was in grade school the whole family had been wondering which congregation I would join.

Nicknames

Nothing kept me still or tied me down. Maybe they called me Maida because they could never get me to stay still long enough to pronounce all of Magdalena. God used my natural interests to draw me closer and closer to him.

In college, I'd do humanitarian work on weekends up in the rural mountain areas with a group of friends. We built houses and set up irrigation systems, but I wasn't doing it for credits for my architecture courses. I loved being up in the mountains with the villagers, living a little of their life with them and in some way meeting Jesus Christ in their needs. Those times motivated me to pray more and better.

Another one of my many natural interests was music. My guitar (Geronima was its name) was my right arm; it went everywhere with me. In high school I hit the music scene, so to speak. I played the guitar, wrote lyrics and sang; and sometimes my friends and I would go to music festivals and perform. I remember spending hours in my room writing music. It wasn't only self-expression. Writing songs, singing at festivals – all of it became a way for me to grow closer to Christ. Today the passion for music remains. I continue to write and play. Music is still my prayer.

*W*AS *T*HAT *M*Y *N*AME *I* *H*EARD?

My first encounter with the Legionaries of Christ led me to discern God's will for my life. It was God's providence that brought them into my life.

In the last year or two of high school, I started looking for ways to live my faith more actively. When I started college, I headed straight to the pastoral department. It happened that just that year, the Legionaries had been put in charge of it.

Through the Legionaries, I met the Regnum Christi

Movement. Regnum Christi fascinated me from the very first moment I joined it. It had what I was looking for: fidelity to the Church, love for the Pope, charity and apostolic zeal.

My involvement in Regnum Christi brought my spiritual life to a higher level. I began receiving the sacraments more frequently: going to daily Mass and confession once a month. My prayer life began to mature and a spiritual thirst grew in my soul.

Whispers

It was a beautiful summer day in February of 1986. (Remember, Chilean summer is during the Northern Hemisphere's winter.) Regnum Christi was starting an elementary school and some friends and I had volunteered to help out.

Making our way to the future kindergarten we surveyed the boring monochrome walls – those would have to be the first to go. We pried open our paint cans and got to work.

When about three of the classrooms were covered with painted ducks and rainbows, a group of four young women walked in and invited us to break for lunch. None of us had ever met them before, but their smiles and the promise of food were welcomed. We were starving.

Over lunch and coffee, they introduced themselves as consecrated women of Regnum Christi. They'd arrived in Chile the day before and would be working in the school when it opened. Even though I'd been a Regnum Christi member for four years,

I'd never heard about the consecrated women. Maybe someone had mentioned something about them, but I never made a connection.

That was the first of many meetings. I did not want to admit it, but as time passed I was growing more and more attracted to the consecrated women and their way of life. When I did my morning prayers or went to Mass I could feel that Christ wanted more from me. It made me nervous. I started to pray just a little less and only go to Mass every other day, excusing myself. It's true that I was busy, but this had never influenced my spiritual life before.

I had to face the fact that I felt a call to the consecrated life; a call that began with my name: "Magdalena." But I could not bear to listen to it. I did not want to talk about it.

Finally, I turned to Our Lady. I entrusted my discernment to her and prayed a Hail Mary everyday, for six months, asking her to help me follow God's will. I loved Christ too much to let him down, but I didn't see what God wanted clearly. So for those six months I begged Our Lady for her guidance and I never went to bed without saying my Hail Mary.

A *C*ALL, AND AN *A*NSWER

In April I went on a retreat, and my heart seemed more open. In prayer and during Mass I saw Christ's call more clearly, but I still refused to acknowledge it openly to anyone. I was afraid – maybe that they would pressure me into following the call, or dissuade me from it: it was something that I both wanted very much and at the same time didn't want at all.

A week after the retreat, my resolve broke. I needed to sort things out, but I could not do it by myself, so I went to my spiritual guide, a consecrated woman, for help. I slowly stammered out that I thought I might have a vocation. For as nervous as I was, her response both surprised me and gave me a great sense of peace. She didn't try to push me into the chapel to make my promises, or tell me that I was imagining things. She simply gave me two bits of advice: be open to God's will, and build a stronger prayer life. What a relief!

A Personal *I*nvitation

Around the same time I had met the Legionaries (during my freshman year at college), I'd also met two co-workers from Mexico. Their joy and zeal attracted me, and I decided that I would give two years as a co-worker once I finished college.

Of course when I made that decision I was under the impression that it would only take me five years to finish college. I did not realize that I would switch majors halfway through. That meant starting school all over again as a freshman - five more years to finish my degree. I kept the idea in the back of my mind, but surely it was God's plan that I would wait until I had finished school. Up until that point my plans and God's had seemed to fit so perfectly.

May of 1986: things took a bit of a turn. A friend came up to me and said:

"Magdalena, what are you doing for the next 12 months? You and I should be co-workers starting now."

Ridiculous. I still had two years of school left.

"You know…" I began. And then I replied: "You know, you're probably right."

I could hardly believe the words were leaving my mouth! I was agreeing with her!

Be realistic, Magdalena, I told myself, you know you don't have the money, and there's probably no way you'll get the time off school…

*C*ALLING *T*HINGS *B*Y *T*HEIR *R*EAL *N*AME…

Everything about being a co-worker worked out. Amazingly, my parents offered to help out with the expenses and the university agreed to hold my credits for two years. Things were going in the right direction, but don't get the impression that it was easy.

My co-worker assignment was to Madrid, Spain. I had never been away from my family before, and Spain, for as nice as it was, wasn't Chile. I missed my family and friend and country so badly. I began to cry before I even got on the plane.

"Maida, are you going to come back?" my father asked me with a worried look as they called my boarding group.

"Of course, Dad," I hastened to reassure him. Of course I would come back to Chile, but we both knew that that wasn't what he meant.

CALL WAITING

Someone told me once that if "you give God your hand, he'll grab your arm and leg too." How true. Looking back now I can see how I thought becoming a co-worker would serve as an escape hatch from the vocation. In some ways it was. But Christ's call, "come, follow me," still echoed in my mind. I was giving Christ two years while he was awaiting the opportunity to ask me for more. Once I arrived in Spain, he grabbed his opportunity: spiritual exercises, an eight day silent retreat. It sounded a little intimidating, but by the grace of God, I decided to go.

I had been seriously considering a vocation for six months. Christ had been working in my soul. Now, alone with him in a silent retreat, I could not avoid the echo of his voice calling me. Only I wanted to be sure, and the whole thing was so uncertain.

As the retreat progressed from day to day, I could hear him more clearly. I kept telling him:

"Show me. I need to see. I need an answer. If I really know that consecrated life is your will for me then I'll get consecrated, but I'm not sure."

On the fifth day of the retreat I got the chance to go to confession.I confessed every sin I could possibly think of, but I still had a dread feeling that I should tell the priest about my difficulty in discerning my vocation. I said the whole thing from beginning to end and waited for an answer.

Silence.

Finally after some time had passed he said:
"After all that you've told me, you still don't know?"
The words were like a lightning bolt. I knew. I really knew.

I needed to pray, to think, to ... go for a walk.

I picked up my notebook of retreat notes, and as I flipped through the pages, my eyes fell on something I'd written about the rich young man in the Gospel. He had said to Christ:
"Good Teacher, what must I do to inherit eternal life?" I read Christ's response: "Why do you call me good? Go sell what you have ... and come follow me."
(cf Mark 11:17-22)

Christ answered a question with a question. Then like a sunrise, slow and clear, it dawned on me. All this time I'd been asking Christ:
"How do I know? What should I do? What do you want?"
I wanted an answer, but I did not realize that Christ was asking me a question:
"Magdalena, will you sell all that you have and come follow me? Will you help me save souls? Will you give your entire life for love of me as I gave my life for you?"

He was calling me by my name, and looking on me with the same love as he did the rich young man.

Yes. I could only say yes.

This sudden understanding was my sign. Christ gave me his peace. After six months of praying my Hail Mary's every night for her help, she answered my prayer on that August 22, 1986, the Feast of the Coronation of Mary.

At one moment I heard God calling my name and I saw my vocation before me as clear as the sun on a cloudless day. I've never doubted it, even though the clouds have sometimes hidden the sun's light. But a vocation is to follow that sun I once saw, even when I can no longer feel its warmth or see it shining.

My sixteen years of consecrated life have been full: full of tears, of joys, of difficulties and of triumphs. My life is full, because it is full of God's love, and my heart is at peace because it knows what true happiness is. I have heard my real name.

SOMETHING MORE

Mariana Ibáñez

*M*y father died when I was nine. It was sudden – an accident – and, just as suddenly, life changed. Dad's chair in the dining room was empty; there was no Dad to run to early on Sunday morning and pounce on to wake up. The only things left of Dad were the smell of him on his sweatshirt and the tapes he'd left behind that no one else liked to listen to. My dad, the man who had taken me on an early morning run that day, and had let me sit on his tummy while he read me the comic strips and watched the football game, the man I had hugged that morning after he cut off a rose bud from the garden… he was now gone. Only an ache, a lonely, empty space that I couldn't explain was left.

I think I changed, after that. I had been a bit of a tomboy before, disorganized and mischievous, the despair of my mother but Dad's little girl. I never worried much about anything. I didn't lose that part of me because my dad died. The experience made me discover something new about myself, or about God. God was close to me, like he is always close to people who are suffering. I knew he was near me, that I could talk to him. I could trust him. I could tell him everything and he would understand.

It wasn't that I couldn't tell Mom anything, or that she

spent all day moping around the house. She never cried in front of us children but I didn't want to make things any harder for her, so I kept my questions for God.

One ordinary evening, as I looked at her over the dinner table serving us our meal, listening to stories about our day at school, hearing my teen-age brothers complain about not being able to go to some party, I perceived something in her that I hadn't before. She was all alone.

I left the table and went up to my room. I sat on my bed and began to think about things. I don't know who it was that I made the promise to, to her – or to God – or maybe to my Dad, but I would never do anything to hurt Mom. I would spend my life trying to please and make her happy. And my Dad, too, looking down from heaven: I wanted to make him proud. I promised that I would try to study to be smart like Dad was, I would train to be an athlete like he was; I would try to be obedient and to be grown-up; I would never leave Mom's side.

But all the time, I think that God was telling me: "Don't rely on those you love most. Rely on me."

A Woman for Others

"We're going to Dallas," Mom announced one morning, all of a sudden.

I, now fourteen, put down my coffee cup.

"We're not moving again," I said.

"They asked us to go and help to start up a school."

"In Dallas? In the United States?"

"I already said that, Mariana."

"But you never asked me."

Moving from Mexico to Spain was one thing – we'd done that shortly after Dad's death so that we could go back to be with Mom's family – but Spain to the U.S.? Another move? A new language, new people, beginning over again …? I was happy where I was, with my friends, with my school and our apartment.

On the plane, I was by myself in an aisle seat, staring out the window at the Atlantic Ocean underneath us. We had flown from Madrid to Paris and were on our way to New York to catch yet another flight to Dallas. It was so unfair. We were going to a place where I would not know anything or anyone – the language, the people, the food, the fashion, nothing.

And then I thought of my dad.

I remembered on one of those morning runs, as I panted trying to keep up, he had explained something to me about his work:

"Mariana, you know there's always something good wherever you go. You just have to try and make the best out of it."

I made the decision, as the stewardess was approaching with the drinkcart, that I would try to make the best out of it. I sealed the decision with a diet Coke.

MEETING UP WITH...

"Oh come on, Mariana," Tracey said tossing her hair. "It's not like it's so bad."

We were planning for the prom. There were roughly three thousand ideas for the theme and Tracey and I were sorting through them, but they were all so girly.

"We could do something more fun," I said. "I don't know – something like a world – you know."

"I still like the sea idea."

"It's so 'Little Mermaid' though..."

"Oh, come on. You're such a boy, Mariana." I made a face, and Tracey laughed at me. "Don't worry, Brian doesn't think so." Brian was my boyfriend.

"Okay, I forgive you," I said.

"I still like the sea idea. It would be so different. Plus your prom dress is going to match."

"Tracey, dark blue matches with everything."

Moving to the States was only awful for about a month, and after that, everything fell into place. I was doing okay at school, I had good friends, track was going well, and I had an incredible boyfriend. I was happy. Sort of. I was restless inside. I felt like I should be doing more, like I could be helping more – but how?

That was when I met two people who showed me the secret to happiness.

The phone rang one evening during my freshman year. It was one of Mom's friends.

"Don't spread the word," the voice on the other end of the phone said, "but you are invited to a private Mass with Mother Teresa tomorrow."

The Missionaries of Charity were inaugurating a home in Dallas for unwed mothers and Mother Teresa of Calcutta would be coming for the grand opening.

"Be good," Mother Teresa smiled and patted me on the face. She was a miniscule old woman, but she still managed to fill the whole room as she made her way through it, smiling and talking to the people eager to meet her. I stood watching her. There was something – but it was hard to describe. I didn't have any idea what a saint was; but I saw in her someone who was really happy, the way I wanted to be.

The second person who showed me real happiness was Pope John Paul II. This was a little more long distance.

"What's your name?" asked a pretty girl with thick eyeliner and long straight dark hair.

"Mariana," I said.

We were sitting, waiting for our bags to come off the airplane and be sorted onto the baggage wheel. All of us looked faded from the long flight.

She grinned at me.

"This is going to be amazing. I can't believe we're going to be able to see the Pope."

I just nodded. I wasn't incredibly excited about that; but she seemed to be.

"My name's Yvette, by the way."

"You're in Regnum Christi, right?"

"Yes; what about you?"

"My mom is."

"Is that how you heard about World Youth Day in Compostela?"

It definitely wasn't my idea to spend a month of the summer on a pilgrimage to World Youth Day in Santiago de Compostela, Spain. Again, without consulting me, Mom had bought the ticket and signed me up to go on a World Youth Day pilgrimage with Regnum Christi. Travelling sounded great but I was uncomfortable at the thought of spending a whole month with people I'd never met. What would they be like? Would I fit in? Would they be weird? Would they think I was weird? Would I have fun or just spend the month waiting to come home?

"We're going to have the most amazing time," said Yvette again. "I've been waiting all summer for this. The Pope is so awesome; I can't wait to see him! We really have to pray to soak it all up."

She jumped up to get her bags off the conveyer belt. This was something new. I'd never met a person my age who talked so openly about praying – or was so enthusiastic about the Pope.

The others were the same. They were a close group that knew and got along with each other. I soon felt included, accepted and considered. Everyone was so open and natural. The interest and friendship they showed were real. Nobody talked badly about anyone else - first surprise. Nobody tried to pretend they were someone else - second surprise. We were real friends. It was the beginning of the most amazing time, as Yvette had said.

We made it, like the medieval pilgrims, to Santiago de

Compostela. It was the night of the prayer vigil, and there I was with my candle, huddled close to the rest of the group in the field. We were surrounded by hundreds and thousands of other young Catholics, who prayed, sang and talked until the moment the Holy Father arrived. The TV projected his face on the big screen, and there, I saw the same "something different" in him as I had in Mother Teresa. I was silent, straining to hear his voice echoing over the loudspeakers.

"… and Christ was a man for others," said the Pope.

"A man for others." What did that mean? I wondered. I had been discovering Christ as a true friend on the pilgrimage. He was a man for others; a man for me, and he was inviting me to be his friend.

"No one has more love than he who gives his life for his friends."

Yes, I thought, I want to love you, and you are my friend, but where am I supposed to start?

*Y*OU *H*AVE *M*ADE *U*S *f*OR *Y*OURSELF, *O L*ORD ...

I didn't have to wait long for an answer. It was my last year of high school and in order to graduate, I had to complete a certain number of service hours. I volunteered with the Missionaries of Charity in that home for unwed mothers where I'd met Mother Teresa. I spent my Friday nights for the next six weeks cleaning, sorting donations of food and baby formula and befriending the girls who went there for help. Mopping floors wasn't as glamorous as going out with my boyfriend or winning a track meet — but I would drive home happier after an evening of volunteering than any of those other times. Even after I had completed my service hours, I continued going back to help.

"So, what are you doing next year?"

It was right before a meet. Jaimie and I were warming up on the field. I groaned inside: the "Senior Year Question" again. Couldn't people think of something else to talk about?

"I'm not sure yet," I said coolly, and turned around to stretch a different muscle.

It was true. Everything I thought of seemed to not be "the everything" that I wanted to do. I wanted to get into international relations like my dad. I wanted to be a track star. If I kept training, next year I could make it for the Olympics. I wanted to study science and math at college. I wanted to serve more, and help more people. I wanted to…

The more I mulled the issue over, the more I saw that what I most wanted to do, before I did anything else, was to give something back to God. He had given me so much: my good health, my family, my faith, my friends. I asked myself: what can I do to pay him back for all of this? I am so small. What could I give to him? The words I had heard at World Youth Day suddenly came back to mind:

"No one has greater love than to lay down one's life for one's friends."

My life. I had my life. Couldn't I give him a little of it? Yes, I could. I decided to be a co-worker.

Mom supported me, and as for my boyfriend Brian, giving up a year in missionary work as a Regnum Christi co-worker didn't seem to pose any major obstacles to our plans. We were sure that we'd get married later. Waiting a year would make the relationship mature.

I saved up my money, bought a couple of big suitcases and booked my plane ticket. I was going to give God a year.

*A*ND *O*UR *H*EARTS *A*RE *R*ESTLESS...

Being with the other co-workers was like being with the group of friends I'd made at World Youth Day – the same real friendship. However, getting to know the consecrated women was something new. They intrigued me. There was something about them. I'd wake up before all the other co-workers, get ready quickly and slip into the back of the chapel to listen to them pray their morning prayers. Serenity would settle in as I listened to the Gregorian chant of the 'Veni Creator' (Come, Holy Spirit) before beginning their meditation. Longing arose in my heart, but I held back from sharing it with anyone else. Since my father's death, I tried never to burden others with my concerns.

My co-worker assignment was in Barcelona, Spain. Living side-by-side with the consecrated, watching them work and pray and interact with each other made me ask myself why they were so happy, so really happy, the way I had seen Mother Teresa happy? Why did I feel so at peace and at home with them? Why was I happier now than I had ever been?

I never said anything about it, because I feared another question that lurked in my soul: could God call me? But the questions kept bothering me so much that I finally confided in my spiritual guide.

"Mariana," she said, "Don't worry, God will give you an answer. Be open to him and trust he'll show you his will and give you the strength to follow it."

The end of my co-worker year came too quickly and the question was still there, in my conscience like a prodding finger. Did God want me to be… consecrated? I couldn't leave without knowing.

"Mom," I said into the receiver, "I've decided to give another year."

Static silence. Then Mom's voice from the other side of the Atlantic:

"Really, Mariana, another year? You're going to get married, aren't you? And how are you going to tell Brian?"

How was I going to tell Brian? What would I say? 'Hope you don't mind waiting another year until I find out if I'll come back or leave you for good?'

"Well…" I crossed my fingers and prayed that he'd found someone else. I knew that he had been dating a few other people over the past year: "Maybe he's found someone else, Mom."

"The least you can do is to tell him yourself."

"I'm coming home for the summer, Mom. Remember?"

I wasn't looking forward to that summer. I was flying across the Atlantic for the fifth time in my life to spend the summer at home with my family – and to break the news to Brian.

The moment came for our "big" conversation. I was so happy to see him again, but at the same time my stomach was tied in knots. I hoped he would say: "I've found someone else." We sat down to dinner and searched through the menu for the silliest dishes we could choose. We laughed about the lobster cassoulet and the description of a roast beef sandwich like usual. I loved looking at him, seeing him again, laughing with him – and at the same time, I was so afraid. The question clouded the dinner – I didn't want to ask him or to tell him, but I knew I had to. I wanted to give God the first chance in my life.

The waitress took our orders and removed the glossy menus.

"Mariana," he said finally, serious now, looking at me. "I've been waiting till you came home to tell you this. You know that I've been dating some other girls, and I'm more sure of this than I ever have been - you're the only one. I want to marry you."

Oh Lord, why? Please tell me this isn't really happening.

I looked down at my plate.

Did I really have to do this? I thought to myself. Maybe this is a sign that God wants Brian and I together. I'll kill him if I tell him. I can't, I can't do this to him.

Mariana … my conscience spoke up.
"I'm sorry," I said. "I've decided to give another year."

His face fell and I could see all the disappointment inside him, but he only nodded and looked away for a moment. Then he turned to me and said:

"Are you sure?"

"Yes."

"Okay. Okay. If you want to wait, I'll wait for you."

... *U*NTIL *T*HEY *R*EST IN *Y*OU

"Mariana, it's so good to have you back!"

I didn't think so. Returning to Barcelona was something I both desired and dreaded. It seemed like everyday I would feel the pull of Christ's call more strongly, but everyday the thought of my mom and of Brian and of all my dreams would pull me in the other direction with equal intensity.

I could no longer deny it that Christ was calling me, but could I say yes? Could I really do what I had to do in order to follow him? Do something that I knew would hurt the people I loved most?

God knew the hurt I was going through, even though at times I thought he couldn't understand how painful it was. As the weeks in Barcelona passed by, he gave me constant gifts of love and reassurances of his presence. There were small signs: Gospel passages that invited me to trust in his grace, good advice given to me in confession, a sense of peace and security when I prayed before the Blessed Sacrament. And there were big signs as well.

One afternoon, two co-workers and I were helping out at a retreat in a local parish. We knew that this particular parish was not the most "orthodox," but we figured that was all the more reason to offer our help. We expected some of the activities to be a little bit different from what we were used to, but nothing could have prepared us for what took place during the Mass.

The décor and the readings were strange, and we felt uncomfortable from the beginning of the Mass,but at the offertory we started glancing nervously at each other. Instead of bringing up unleavened wafers for the consecration, an ordinary loaf of bread was laid on the altar; a valid but illicit way of celebrating the Eucharist.

"This is my Body."

I watched in disbelief as the loaf was passed around for each communicant to tear off his own piece. Crumbs fell from hands onto sweaters and were shaken off onto the carpet. I couldn't believe it. Christ was present in every bit of that bread and was now strewn about the floor.

As soon as the retreatants left for lunch the co-workers and I fell to our knees to gather up the scattered pieces of the Blessed Sacrament. Christ's humility was too much for me. He was allowing himself to be literally trampled upon. There, touching my finger to my tongue to pick up the crumbs, I prayed as I never had before. It was a simple prayer, but it came from the depths of my heart.

"Jesus, these people are good people. They wouldn't be setting a day aside for you if they weren't looking for you. But no one has ever told them that you are here in the Eucharist. That's why they threw you on the ground. I am sure that I have often stepped on you and brushed you away; not physically, but spiritually, because Lord, I am stubborn and selfish and blind.

"I am so sorry, Christ, please forgive me. If my poor, weak and simple life could in any way serve you or help you to touch even just one of these souls, if my life in turn would be for you a consolation, if my heart given to you could be an instrument, then ... take me, Lord.

"Here I am. Take my life."

I had done it. I had offered him my entire heart. Why had I made Christ wait so long? I suppose I had expected that the moment of saying yes would be something cataclysmic, heart wrenching, painful and dramatic. It wasn't. It was simple and sweet and silent and left me overwhelmed with peace and joy.

From then on, prayer stopped being the torture it had been for the past year. When I prayed, I no longer felt like I was playing tug of war, or fighting a lost cause with someone who wanted to make my life miserable. I no longer saw Christ as my opponent, but rather, as a most loving partner. It was like falling in love. Everyday I discovered something new about him, something that made me more convinced about him and about my vocation.

However, this newfound feeling of nearness to Christ didn't take away the sacrifice. Every decision implies a renunciation. I thought a lot about my mom and about my boyfriend. I had to break the news, to say goodbye, and to leave. Were it not for the grace of God and strength I received from prayer, I would never have been able to do what to me seemed impossible.

Telling my mom was the hardest thing I have ever done. My heart broke to see her cry. She wanted an explanation, she wanted certainties and she didn't want to lose me. But, just as God was guiding me, he was strengthening her. She didn't understand at first, but she gave me all the support that she could.

Then came Brian. We had gone out to dinner again and were sitting talking over dessert. We talked about college, about some job offers he'd gotten and then he began to talk about the house he was planning for us, and the ring he wanted to buy. It was then that I told him:

"Brian, I can't marry you."

He looked at me in disbelief.

I continued, "I know what I'm going to say is hard and that you might not understand, but I have a vocation and I'm going to get consecrated."

Silence.

"Mariana, – but don't you love me?"

"Yes, you know I do!" I told him, trying to choke back my tears.

"How can you do this?"

How could I explain? I wasn't doing this because I didn't love him, or because I didn't want to get married. I did love Brian, very much, but I knew that Christ was asking this of me, and deep inside, I knew I loved Christ more, and I wanted to belong to him no matter what it cost.

I stayed up late that night, long after Brian had brought me home, crying. It was a deep-felt hurt. All I could do was offer it to Christ.

"Jesus," I prayed, "You know the only reason I did it was for love of you. Help me. Give me your strength. Help Brian to understand. Help Mom, too. Take care of them, Lord."

"Mariana, don't you think I love them more than you do? They are in my hands. I'd never ask you to give them up if I weren't going to take care of them. The closer you are to me, the closer I am to them. Trust in me."

It was the answer to my prayer.

ᔕ

Ten years have gone by since that night. Maybe leaving those I loved was the hardest thing I've ever done, maybe it wasn't, but it was worth it – Christ has been worth it, my vocation and my mission as a consecrated woman in Regnum Christi have been worth it, and I wouldn't change my life for anything.

Christ is my life. After ten years I can attest to the fact that what he promises in the Gospel is true: Whoever leaves father or mother, or boyfriend or a future family or the Olympics for his sake will receive a hundred fold in this life (with suffering) and eternal life as well. It is true. Christ himself is this hundred fold. He is the reward of a consecrated soul. Having him, there is nothing I lack.

*M*ASTER *P*LANS

Margaret Mullan

I tried to ignore my noisy brothers and sisters as they watched the reruns of a classic movie from the 1950s for the hundredth time, and turned back to my algebra equations. Only half a year left of school. I had big plans. I was going to attend an Ivy League University and then go onto become a world-renowned scientist. A member of the Mullan family needed to have great expectations.

The next morning, groggily munching my cereal I stared at the book I was reading.

"Pass the milk, please, Margaret," my mother said.

"Margaret, wake up," said my brother John, elbowing me. I looked up and passed him the milk. John was my role model and hero. Everything John did was 'the best.' In sports, school, friends… One day, I would be just like him.

I passed a note to my friend across the desk, while the teacher was explaining for the umpteenth time the importance of $a^2 - b^2$. The note read:

Frances, R U bored? R U going to youth group meeting 2night?

Frances tugged her hair, about to write back when the teacher stopped in mid-sentence.

"Margaret, what is $a^2 - b^2$?"

"Um," I said, and stared at the board as though the problem really worried me. I had no idea.

"Frances?"

She had no idea either. "Pay more attention to class, girls." We nodded and pretended to be writing studiously in our math books. Frances found a moment when the teacher wasn't looking to scribble back the answer.

I'm going 2 youth group. Did U hear the news about the beach trip? 2 good 2 B true.

What beach trip?

"You all need to start fund raising," our youth group leader told us. "Summer's coming and we're going to need it."

"All right," we chorused.

I was definitely looking forward to summer.

The last night of the beach trip, while everyone else was dozing, I was lying on the floor with my head propped up and my eyes riveted on the screen. I was exhausted from a couple days of constant fun, but I was resisting sleep, the movie was too good not to watch. It was about an Irish girl who went to El Salvador to be a missionary. The pictures of the poor, the suffering, the empty and the hungry attacked my heart. When the heroine, Jeannie, went back to Ireland after being threatened by terrorists, I hugged my pillow and half-hoped that she'd get the courage to go back. Couldn't she see they still needed her? Now, standing with tears rolling down her face, and facing her boyfriend, she was saying:

"I choose to die. I choose to give all. What else is this life for?"

And as the camera faded to the next scene. Jeannie was climbing aboard a plane for El Salvador to go back to what she knew could be death. White words scrolled across the TV screen, "Jeannie was never seen again. A week later the missionaries' van was found discarded on the side of the road, without any sign whatsoever of what became of the woman who gave all to help those who had nothing."

I threw my pillow down.

"No!" I shouted

The others started to wake.

"Oh come on, Margaret. Don't be such a baby. It's only a movie…"

I couldn't help it. I was crying and crying. It wasn't because she died – it was because, somewhere inside, the echo of the words came: "Give everything to help those who have nothing." It just wasn't right. It wasn't fair. People needed help — did I have what it took to be the one to give it?

"You're going to bed early," said Mom, when I got home, looking at the rings burnt around my eyes. I lay in bed staring at the ceiling remembering the movie: "Give everything…"

I should be doing something. I could give my clothes to the poor, but then Mom would be mad. I couldn't go to El Salvador. What was I supposed to do? I was only thirteen. And why did it have to be me?

Maybe … maybe after college I'd help. Then I could really give everything.

My Way

Three years later I was in a prestigious high school, studying college level AP courses. I was narrowing down my university selections and deciding on possible majors. Everything was going according to plan. I had the right friends, the right clothes, the right boyfriend and I was on my way to getting into the right college.

Waiting for the college entrance exam to begin, I imagined it all. Princeton, degree, marriage, a reasonably sized family and a good career. This was just the beginning.

"You will have three hours to write your essay," the instructor announced. "Do not turn the page until you are told. Read the instructions completely. You may begin."

I whipped over my sheet and read the essay question.

Nothing. Nervously, I read the question again. Nothing.

The question meant nothing to me. No answers were forthcoming.

'Margaret!' I told myself, trying to remain calm. 'You have been studying this all year long. Get your act together; this is not the time to blank out.' But I couldn't remember anything about the essay question.

Nothing.

Furious and terrified, I read the question again, and then began frantically praying Hail Marys. This couldn't be happening. I HAD to pass this exam; my whole future depended on it!

"Hi, Margaret," John said, opening the car door for me. I got in and slammed it behind me. We headed out of the parking lot.
"Margaret, is something the matter?" John asked.
"It's not fair!" I burst out, starting to cry. "I blanked out, I totally blanked out. And I've been working all year on this. And now – "
"Hey, Margaret, those things happen."
"You don't even understand," I wailed.
"Listen, don't worry, God will take care of it."
"Come on, John," I said, pulling out tissues to wipe my face.
"It's true, I promise. God's in control, he'll take care of your life."
"Oh whatever," I said. I wasn't sure I wanted that.

*L*IKE *B*ROTHER *L*IKE *S*ISTER

I'd always followed John. I listened to him more than most

people, and I tried to imitate everything I saw him do. If he was popular at school, I tried to be; if he was good at sports, I tried to be.

At the end of my tenth grade year and John's high school graduation, he packed up his things, took one last look at our house, our backyard, our old tree house, our dog, and finally us, and then left ... not for college, as I had been expecting.

He left for the seminary.
And he hadn't even told me.

Popular, athletic, intelligent, attractive, influential... Yes. I'd follow him that far. But holy?

And at the same time, I was uneasy, pervaded by disquiet. I wanted more. I wanted to do more. I wanted to help those suffering in our world. I wanted to give everything. I knew deep down that God wanted me to serve others.

But I had my plans made. I told God the same thing I had told him that night three years earlier when I had laid in bed staring at the ceiling, "Maybe after college."

*a W*AKE-UP *C*ALL

Senior year.

On the outside, new friends and a new life. But inside nothing had changed. Maybe it had, a little, because now on my own I would take time to go and be alone with God, but I was never really willing to give him the one thing that I knew that he wanted: my life. My plans.

I had already sent off early applications to my choice colleges. I had no doubts about getting accepted. All of the colleges were prestigious, but Princeton was number one on my list. As I came home one day after school, Mom handed me a letter. It had come in the morning mail. My palms began to sweat as I read the return address: Princeton Office of Undergraduate Admissions. I tore open the envelope and read:

"Dear Miss Mullan:

The Princeton Office of Undergraduate Admission thanks you for your application. ... You have been placed on our waiting list."

Wait-listed?

Impossible.

Didn't they see my SAT scores?

What about the solid 4.0 GPA I had maintained all throughout high school?

What about my AP classes and National Honors Society?

Hadn't they read my references?

I read and re-read the letter until I wadded it up and threw it against the wall. Angry tears filled my eyes. But what could I do about it? Call the admissions office and threaten them? Go there in person and make them eat their words?

For the first time in my life I had been given a 'No', and no amount of studying or resumé writing could change that. Standing there at the kitchen counter I was faced with the realization that I was not all I had thought myself to be. To the rest of the world, and especially to Princeton University, I was just another name among many on a waiting list.

A short while later I found myself sitting down in the living room with Mary, one of the Regnum Christi consecrated women. She always used to stop by our house when she came through the area. We were eating chips and waiting for dinner.

"So, Margaret, how are you?"

"Fine," I said.

"Have you heard back from any of the universities you were applying to?"

"Yes."

"Good news?"

"No," I said.

"Don't worry," said Mary. "I'm sure that God has a plan."

"I'm not so sure," I said.

"Why don't you find out? We have a retreat coming up at Christmas, in Rhode Island. I know it's not too far from you."

A retreat? I needed to think; I needed to talk to God about my plans – and I needed to convince him that they really were the best idea for my life. A retreat would be perfect.

THE HOUND OF HEAVEN

On Christmas morning I was in the chapel at Mass in the

consecrated women's formation center in Rhode Island. From the altar to the floor flowed rows of poinsettias circling a statue of the baby Jesus resting on hay, and behind me I heard the voices of consecrated women singing 'What Child is This?'

Memories of my desires to give my life to others resurfaced. This time, they weren't merely thoughts about "doing something good" for God. I began to think about a vocation. Should I get consecrated? Was God asking me to be one of them, to give my whole life to him? But ... what about college? What about my degree?

"NO. Absolutely not." I was not about to give up my degree.

Consecrated life was totally out of the question.

A few days later, as I was packing up my things to leave, one of the consecrated women tapped on my door.

"Do you need anything?" she asked.

I didn't look up from the gray pajamas I was rolling up in my suitcase.

"I'm fine. Thanks for everything; it was wonderful."

"I'm glad it helped. You know, we have another retreat at Easter."

"Oh, that's nice," I said politely and zipped up my suitcase without giving it a second thought.

The next months were filled with studying, friends and parties. I was miserable. I knew I was hiding from God. The idea of wanting to give more, the restlessness, the constant disquiet tormented me.

'Oh get a grip, Margaret,' I told myself. 'You just need to sort things out. You know what you want, so don't be stupid.' With time and distance, the whole vocation idea would go away, and then I'd be left in peace to finally start doing what I wanted to.

But try as I might, I couldn't get a grip. Christ was knocking insistently. I would constantly hear his voice in songs on the radio and in CDs, which I listened to at full volume to drown out his whisper.

Unconciously, though, I must have been waiting for opportunities to hear his voice. I found myself in Rhode Island once again at another retreat during Holy Week. However I had been offered a four-year college scholarship. It seemed that God's plans and my plans were on the same track. Holy Week should just confirm it.

The talks were fine, the atmosphere was nice, the silence was silent, and I liked the others girls on the retreat.

The priest directing the retreat was offering spiritual direction to those interested, and for one reason or another I decided to go. I started off by telling him about my scholarship and my plans and about how well I'd be able to help the Church once I had my degree and was more qualified.

"Have you ever considered a vocation?" he asked.

Hadn't he been listening to all I'd said?

"A vocation?" I replied trying not to let my indignation show. "That's my older brother – he's already in the seminary. I'm thinking more about my future in chemistry…"

He nodded calmly and went on.

I left for home again in a rush, but I couldn't forget the whole "vocation issue."

So I compromised.

Two months later, I was back in Rhode Island, volunteering my time at a summer camp the consecrated women were running in one of their schools.

The last week of the camp, after many of the girls had already left, I took a few free minutes go down to the edge of the property where it overlooked the ocean. After a month of giggling girls and endless hours of sports tournaments, I wanted to be alone.

"How are you doing, Margaret?"

I looked up to see my spiritual guide standing near me. She took a seat on the grass, and in silence we both watched the waves roll over the rocks.

"Okay," I answered her staring at the waves swell in the distance. I wanted to tell her that I wasn't really in the mood for talking. She knew a little bit about my vocational struggle and I was sure she'd try to bring up the subject, but I was determined not to budge an inch on the issue.

"You're doing okay?" she asked, raising her eyebrows. "What are you thinking about?"

"School."

"School? You don't want to give the candidacy a try first?"

"Oh, I'd give the candidacy a try, it's just that I don't know what my parents would say…"

Liar. My parents would support whatever I chose to do, but I had to evade this topic somehow.

"Why not ask them?"

"Because giving candidacy a try means I'd hear it," I burst, and then went silent again when she asked:

"Hear what?"

"I don't know… and anyway my parents… and my scholarship…"

She nodded, and smiled at me.

"You know I'll be praying for you, Margaret."

What was that supposed to mean?

I left Rhode Island like an angry porcupine, spines up. I knew I was making the wrong decision, but I was too proud to admit it.

RUNNING ON EMPTY

"Margaret, what is wrong with you?"

For the hundredth time, I had left a party in tears. It was the last month of my freshman year at college, and the last party of my freshman year. I had firmly promised myself that this, my last party, would be the first that I would get through completely, enjoying myself. But it didn't happen.

Once I had given Christ what I thought was the final no,

I went in the opposite direction. 'You're not doing anything that everybody else on campus isn't doing,' I told myself. Yet the more I tried to convince myself that I loved the socializing, the drinking, the parties, the more empty and miserable I felt.

That summer I tried to find some consolation in the Great Outdoors. With only eighty dollars in my pocket, my sister, Adam (a guy-friend of ours) and I set out cross-country. Even there, on the interstate, with the music blaring, I heard only the echoing of emptiness. One night, in the middle of Pennsylvania, at eleven o'clock at night, we pulled off the road and climbed to the top of a hill. The stars dripped silver in the vast black sea above. We turned our faces to the sky and drank its beauty in. Adam whispered reverently:

"Isn't it beautiful?"

"I want to leave a mark even brighter and more magnificent," I said.

He was confused. It wasn't the answer he expected.

"Let's keep going." I said, and shook myself off as I climbed up from the grass.

"*H*EAR, *O D*AUGHTER..."

The following year I roomed with my two sisters. I was tired of the "frat party" scene, and grateful to be close to my family again. My sisters helped me get back to Mass and to confession, two things I'd neglected during freshman year.

"Oh Mom, it's beautiful!"

It was my twentieth birthday and I was at home for the

weekend. Mom had decided to take me shopping so we could spend some time alone before I returned to school. As we got in the car to head home, she pulled out a little box containing my birthday present: a unique ring, a red ruby in the middle surrounded by six diamonds. It was a family heirloom that had been in her possession for a long time. Her mother had given it to her, and she was now giving it to me.

"It's a special ring, Margaret — the red ruby signifies something that God will ask from you that is going to be very painful. But the six diamonds represent the happiness that will outshine your suffering."

"Mom," I said, "you've no idea how much this means to me." And I don't really think she did at the time. But I saw in it a renewed call from Christ, and while I was not yet ready to tell him yes, at least I was back on speaking terms with him.

One day, as I had become in the habit of doing, I visited the little chapel on campus. I knelt down in front of the tabernacle and opened my Bible.

"Hear, o daughter; consider and incline your ear;
forget your people and your father's house. The King will
desire your beauty. Since he is your Lord, bow to him…"
(Psalm 45[44]:10 - 11)

I knew what the passage meant. I knew what Christ was telling me through it. I couldn't help it – I began to cry, and in the tears I told him:

"Yes, Lord, yes. I'll get consecrated … but after I finish my degree."

As I had done some years earlier, I headed to Rhode Island to get myself together and intelligently plan for my final year of college with a retreat.

The consecrated women were surprised to find me back on their doorstep, but they welcomed me warmly as they always had done, and they did everything they could to help me have a good retreat.

"So, Margaret, what is Christ telling you?" my spiritual guide asked as we went for a walk down the long driveway.

"I think I have a vocation. He's been asking me for a long time, and I've been running. But I'll do it. First, though, I want to get my degree."

"Margaret," she turned to me. In a tone of seriousness, genuine love and concern she said, "Christ has been merciful enough to keep calling you, and if he's calling you now, it's because he wants you to answer. He's giving you the grace to be generous now. Do you want to risk waiting more time?"

I had never seen it like that before. She was right. Who was I to put God on hold and decide when, if, how I would follow him? I had no right to make him comply with my terms. Christ didn't have to wait for me, or put up with the way I treated him. Before I had angrily fought to make Christ leave me alone; now the thought that I might lose this grace frightened me.

*T*AKING THE *S*TEPS

I spent the next year working as a teacher to pay off my

loans. The following summer I entered the candidacy program.

It was drastically different from the way I was used to living: following a schedule and times of silence were hard to get used to. But I soon forgot about those things. I was focused on Christ. I had never met him before as I met him now. He was someone real and alive. I could talk to him about my worries, about my dreams, about my past, about my future. I could cry before him in the Blessed Sacrament and not feel ashamed. I could say "I love you" and not be afraid. In every Mass, every prayer, every verse of the Gospel I read during that summer, I felt Christ, saying, "I love you" to me in return. I knew he meant it. It was something he had wanted to tell me for so long, but I was always too selfish and scared to listen to him.

I opened my heart. I let go of myself. I let go of my plans. Even though I was giving up everything I had ever wanted, I wanted this more than anything.

I said yes to Christ forever on August 29, 1997.

✑

Sometimes they say that if you want to make God laugh, just tell him your plans. Yet, looking back, I'm the one laughing.

My mom was right. Leaving behind my plans to follow my vocation is like the red ruby of sacrifice, but it is a sacrifice surrounded by the diamonds of Christ's love, his peace and his faithfulness .

*f*ind out more about us @

www.regnumchristi.org

www.vocation.com

www.shorelines.com

*f*ollow me

Matthew 4:19

*V*ocation *D*irector
60 Austin Ave,
Greenville,
Rhode Island 02828

Ph: 877-866-7738
        401-378-3201
Fax: 401-949-5681
email: matere@ids.net

*J*esus *C*hrist himself called
the first men and women to totally consecrate
their lives to him.
Throughout 20 centuries, he has continued
to make the same call in every generation.
Each woman consecrated to him in Regnum Christi has
heard his call and left everything to follow him.

Following *C*hrist:
"who, virginal and poor, redeemed and sanctified men by obedience unto death on the cross," (Vatican II, Perfectae Caritas), we live the three evangelical counsels:

C H A S T I T Y:
We exclusively dedicate ourselves to the sole
and supreme love of Christ. We joyfully and
freely embrace celibacy, renouncing the state
and benefits of marriage.

P O V E R T Y:
We only possess one thing: the crucifix we
receive on the day of our consecration. This total
poverty frees us from the ties to the world,
enabling our total availability for the mission of
spreading Christ's Kingdom until he reigns in
the heart of every person and in society.

O B E D I E N C E:
We put our understanding and will at the
service of God's plan, expressing in the most
concrete way our complete dedication to the
one we love. His will guides every minute of
our lives.

PER REGNUM CHRISTI AD GLORIAM DEI

for the Kingdom of Christ to the Glory of God